Ice, Fire, and Blood

Norman Black

AUTHOR'S NOTE

A sequel to *Ice, Fire, and Blood,* will recount experiences of GIs in civilian life, after, combat duty in the Korean War.

One Moment in Annihilation's Waste,

One Moment, of the Well of Life to taste—

The Stars are setting and the Caravan

Starts for the Dawn of Nothing

Oh, make haste!

Rubáiyát 38, by Omar Khayyám,

as translated by Edward Fitzgerald

CONTENTS

ACKNOWLEDGMENTS

I am grateful to many men whose names, usually last names only, I knew but briefly while we drank coffee during class-breaks and after classes of evening-college courses we took at the U.S. Army base in Yokohama, Japan, in 1957. The stories they told, about their combat experiences during the Korean War form the story's warp and woof.

The late Maj. William A. McClain, AUS Ret. of Norcross, Gwinnett County, Georgia, and Wiley Virden of Atlanta, Georgia, both of whom served in combat with infantry during the Korean War, also told me valuable information that influenced what I wrote. Col. Robert E. Harrison, AUS Ret. of Glasgow, Kentucky, who served with the U.S. Army's Judge Advocate General Corps, gave me information that helped me to avoid including a major error in the story. I appreciate the time each took to talk with me.

I am grateful to Monica Walsh, curator of research of the RAAF Museum at Cook Point, Victoria, Australia, for information about and photos of the RAAF's 77 Squadron Mustang aircraft, which flew in support of US and allied troops very early in the Korean War. In connection with this long-distance research, I also want to thank James Martin, senior historical officer in the museum's Office of Air Force History.

I extend my gratitude also to Robert E. Richardson, division director of the Special Media Archives Services Division of the

National Archive and Records Administration (NARA), in College Park, Maryland and his staff: especially Holly Reed of Still Picture Reference. With Ms. Reed's help and that of others at NARA, I was able to find images of action, weapons, and weapon systems in use during the time covered by this book.

I am also indebted for careful readings and valuable critiques of the book's manuscript and its sequels, which were done by the late Richard Y. Haver, a World War II, Pacific Theater infantry veteran and my former bureau chief, at the *Newark (NJ) Evening and Sunday News*; his wife Wilma; and Mary "Mayna" Cosby, all of North Charleston, South Carolina. Charlotte Petrides of Chamblee, Georgia and Charlotte Walker of Atlanta, Georgia each also carefully read and critiqued the manuscript, and I am equally grateful to them for the careful thought they gave the story's flow and content and the many useful suggestions they made.

The manuscript was also read by Judge Ben Smith, Jr. of Waycross, Georgia, who was awarded the Purple Heart for a wound received during his service in World War II. He pointed out numerous errors, including military usage and also suggested several names for the work, which resulted in the present title. I am most grateful to him for the time he spent and thought he gave the task. I am also indebted to James V. Carroll, assistant editor of *The American Legion Magazine* and Arthur G. Sharp, editor of *The Graybeards*, the Korean War Veterans Association's magazine, for reading the manuscript and commenting about it.

Lastly and very importantly, I want to thank Janie McQueen of Cumming, Georgia, a former newspaper reporter, for encouragement and advice that led to this work's publication. The manuscript had languished, until she encouraged me to publish it. She also did a final proofreading of the manuscript, formatted it for publication, and nudged me to find relevant photos for use with it. Without her encouragement and help, the manuscript would have remained in a storage box.

With all the help I got, the reader will understand that if there are any factual errors in the book they are my fault.

Norman Black

Marietta, Cobb County

Georgia

FOREWORD

Ice, Fire, and Blood is about what happened to typical combat infantrymen fighting in Korea during the period from late November 1950 until early spring 1951.

It is a belated result of stories told me by soldiers and marines who fought in Korea while I was on duty with the US Navy in Japan during 1956 and 1957. Since then, I gathered additional firsthand information through conversations and interviews with Korean War veterans. I have woven both the earlier and more recent stories into a composite story. The book's characters are also composites of real men and fictional in that sense only.

If the story seems to highlight men from Dixie that were part of the regular army at that time, it is because Dixie was over-represented in the ranks, when compared with its percentage of the US population. That was because there were many poor, unemployed and under-employed men in Dixie, and poor and underemployed men always filled the US military's enlisted ranks.

One major aspect I have left out is the frequent profanity and derogatory terms for enemies, which men used to express emotions, frustrations, and hopes. I have included such words only where I reckoned them very necessary to show an unusual degree of emotional venom.

The Korean War may be divided into several phases, in which the discipline and equipment of the US Army, and the tactics and strategy of US-United Nations (UN) forces, varied greatly. This book begins in November 1950, during the phase that began with the Inchon landing on September 15, 1950. It ends in mid-1950, before the war entered its final period of stalemate and fixed-position, trench warfare similar to World War I, on the Western Front.

In November 1950, US and allied troops were spread out on a front that stretched across much of the northernmost Korean peninsula. They were there because North Korea had invaded South Korea in June 1950, and the UN had authorized military action to force the withdrawal of North Korean forces from South Korea.

Many countries sent small units to help, but the army was mainly US with a large South Korean presence. The supreme commander of UN forces was US General of the Army Douglas MacArthur, who commanded from his headquarters in Tokyo, where he was surrounded by an admiring staff.

The US army battalion this story centers on was one of those sent to Korea from Japan, in June 1950. Shortly after it landed, US and South Korean forces were beaten back into a defensive perimeter outside the harbor town of Pusan, in southeastern Korea. In early September 1950, the battalion was taken from the perimeter, along with numerous other army and marine units and landed at Inchon, in northwestern South Korea.

When the Inchon landing was made, most North Korean forces were around the perimeter outside Pusan, attacking US and South Korean forces that remained there.

The Inchon landing surprised the North Korean People's Army (NKPA), which had already suffered serious losses from superior US firepower. Within the perimeter, however, leaders of US forces did not know that their forces were, by that time, superior to the NKPA both numerically and in firepower. They and their troops had been severely demoralized by the savage attacks of wave after wave of artillery-supported NKPA infantry and armor, and no intelligence was available to give them a true assessment of the situation.

After the Inchon landings, most NKPA forces around the perimeter retreated northward very rapidly and in good order. With US forces fanning out from Inchon and others pursuing them northward from the Pusan perimeter, the NKPA moved northward on foot, through roadless valleys in the peninsula's central mountains. Most retreated back into North Korea, but some remained in South Korea in the central mountains, and carried out disruptive actions behind US forces.

The US pursuers, from Inchon and the perimeter, were too slow and road-bound to prevent the NKPA's retreat. The NKPA had lost large numbers of men and nearly all its heavy equipment. It units retreated at night and hid successfully each day. Neither US nor UN air forces could stop their retreat, for NKPA forces concealed themselves so expertly they could not be seen from the air.

The NKPA's successful retreat was due not only to poor US tactics, but also to strong communist indoctrination, excellent leadership, and all the discipline needed to maintain unit cohesion and total, unwavering obedience to orders.

US Army forces in Korea had begun the war with obsolete World War II weapons. They were now equipped with the latest weapons, which, until after the Korean War began, had been reserved for US forces in Western Europe. The army's units were also up to organization-table troop levels, although most of the enlisted replacements were fresh out of basic training and combat infantry training. The others were aging non-commissioned officers (noncoms) and officers that had been pulled from comfortable billets in the US and rushed to Korea. None had experienced working together as units.

Once it was clear the NKPA had escaped, Gen. MacArthur proceeded with his own private plan to conquer North Korea and unite it with South Korea, under the rule of Pres. Syngman Rhee, the US-trusted, anti-communist tyrant, who ruled South Korea as his fiefdom.

MacArthur reported to Washington, D.C. that the NKPA had been destroyed as a fighting force. His reports convinced the US government this was true. As a result, the US government was euphoric and allowed MacArthur to set the US' political and military agenda. That was why UN forces were headed northward towards the Yalu River, North Korea's border with China, and, at its far northeastern end, with the Soviet Union (USSR).

UN troops were told the few surviving NKPA troops were retreating towards the Yalu and the extremely rugged and barren mountains there. Once there, they would offer no significant resistance and would possibly retreat into Communist China. By Thanksgiving Day, 1950, there had been no contact with the NKPA for days, and UN forces were certain MacArthur was right.

Each day, as road-bound UN forces moved northward and nearer to the Yalu River, they increased the territory they controlled, and also their distance from their supply sources at Inchon and Pusan. They also increased their certainty the war would be over in a matter of weeks, at most. They moved at a predictable, relatively slow speed, in a predictable direction, along the few, narrow dirt roads, as they followed an enemy as nimble as grasshoppers.

The US military's tanks, anti-aircraft guns, and other mechanized equipment enabled it to concentrate terribly devastating fire on its enemies, but only when those enemies were obliging enough to position themselves in places where US forces could bring that firepower to bear on them. Not only were the UN force's forward movements difficult, but the constant need to re-supply them was also an undertaking of mammoth proportion. In addition to the main north-south road along the eastern coast, there was one main north-south road on the peninsula's western side. The rest were narrow, dirt roads and paths, and there were fewer and fewer of them the farther north one moved.

1

ALMOST OVER

The night was cold and moonless, and so dark it was hard to see twenty feet ahead, much less to the hills that rose on each side of the valley. Corporal Randolf MacKenzie was awake and on guard, in a US-held part of a combat zone in northwestern North Korea, not far north of the Chongchon River.

He was in a foxhole he shared with Private First Class Lamar Darden, who was wrapped in a blanket and asleep, leaning against the other side of the narrow, shallow pit.

It was November 7, 1950, at 0300 hours, the middle of the night. MacKenzie moved slowly and cautiously in the foxhole. He listened carefully for any hint of movement in front or on either side of the position. The murky sky gave no light, for low clouds blotted out the stars, which could at least have shown the outline of the hills.

The foxhole was on the perimeter of the battalion, which, late the evening before, had camped on the swath of barren land between the foot of one hill and the narrow road that led through the valley. The foxhole was situated so as to be part of a covering fire field that interlocked with the other posts to its left and right. But the darkness made that theoretical, since they could not even see the hill's slope or more than a few yards in any direction.

MacKenzie moved his feet enough to keep the blood circulating in them and clenched and unclenched his fingers to keep them from becoming numb from the night's chill. The men were in summer field uniforms, but the night was so cold MacKenzie's breath was white.

MacKenzie's infantry company was at full strength with 190 men, including a two-man Browning automatic rifle (BAR) crew in each platoon. Then, of course, there were the omnipresent heavy trucks, the continual use of which helped the US almost to lose the war.

The company was part of a reinforced infantry battalion that numbered about 2,500 men, which was about what the army's organization table showed it should be. The battalion, in turn, was only one part of a full-strength infantry regiment, in a force consisting of thousands of U.S, Republic of Korea (ROK), and other UN forces moving northward, on the peninsula's western side.

On the eastern side, the peninsula is covered with mountains that rise at steep angles on each side, to razor-like ridges. The peninsula's western side, where MacKenzie's unit was, is also covered with hills, but of more moderate heights, though often extremely steep.

The western valleys sometimes broaden to allow human settlements and agriculture. Sometimes the valleys curve and turn many times in relatively short distances. Along roads in these valleys the UN army moved by day in a constant cloud of dust churned up by its noisy vehicles.

2

RUMBLINGS

Darden moved, or rather, the lumpy blanket next to MacKenzie moved. It was not recognizably Darden until his helmeted head appeared from under it.

"What a hell of a place to be," he whispered. "I don't like anything about this here country. Not even when there ain't no one left to fight."

Lamar Travis Darden was a tall, burly twenty-year-old from northeastern Mississippi. He was neither less nor more unhappy about being in Korea than the rest of the men. Darden was generally an easy-going soldier. He had a good sense of humor, even when physical conditions were poor. Beyond that, his great joys in the military were shooting his rifle at an enemy he was allowed to kill or maim, and any type of gambling, with dice or cards, which soldiers could play in barracks or field.

MacKenzie did not get the same elevated feeling Darden said he got in a firefight. In firefights MacKenzie's senses were heightened, but he knew it was the adrenalin rush every soldier gets when death is about swinging his scythe swiftly and wildly in all directions. It is the kind of buzz, or heightened awareness, that rivets one's attention on the work at hand and makes one lose all sense of time.

Whether Darden had a super adrenalin rush or was really cool and death defying was a question MacKenzie knew he could not answer. But he knew Darden was a good man to have beside him whenever the enemy attacked them, or when they attacked the enemy. Darden was as much fun to be with in peace as he was reliable to be with when death was about. MacKenzie thought a company of men like Darden could cut their way through any opposition the North Koreans could ever throw at them.

When the battalion was in Japan and Darden won big, at craps or cards, he would pay his debts and use some of the rest of his winnings to buy drinks for everyone in his platoon. It was easy to know Darden had won big, if one entered the Enlisted Men's Club and found a party going on for no apparent reason. On those evenings one could find Darden at the bar with a glass of 7-Up in his hand, happily paying for rounds for everyone present. He did not drink alcohol, for religious and health reasons, but he never denied others the right to enjoy it if they wanted to.

Darden was good at the games he played and lost a lot less money than he won, but with his spending habit, he would come to MacKenzie almost every other month to borrow money. MacKenzie never refused and, come payday, Darden always repaid his debt before trying to turn whatever he had left into his first million.

Darden's abstinence from all alcoholic drink was enough to mark him as very different from other US soldiers. Another trait that differentiated him from nearly every other US soldier in Korea was his deadly accuracy when firing any shoulder weapon in use by the US Army. He also remained fully effective and completely cool no matter how difficult a situation seemed. Shooting down attacking enemy soldiers as they charged to kill him while an enemy tank moved towards him seemed no more emotionally stressful than shooting metal ducks at a carnival, or deer or wild turkeys in the Mississippi woods and underbrush in which he had hunted back home.

He had unusual habits that were evident in Japan. One was that he would go to the base library occasionally and find a quiet corner where he could read the small edition of the Bible he carried in his gear. Another was that he always got up quietly on Sunday mornings and slipped out to the chapel to attend the Protestant worship service.

Darden never bothered anyone else with his belief, and no one said much about his. None of his mess mates ever said more about it than occasionally to mention "Darden's religious nature" when the subject of Darden came up. They reckoned he was all right, and whatever went into making him all right was fine with them.

"Wait!" MacKenzie whispered and put an index finger to his lips to signify silence. "I hear footsteps, but it's hard to know just where they come from."

Darden slowly hoisted himself up and looked out over the foxhole's edge as he placed his rifle in his hands ready to fire.

MacKenzie moved his head from side to side to try to decide how near the sounds were and just where they were. He pointed outside the perimeter and whispered, "There."

Before he could determine exactly where the sounds came from, figures emerged from the darkness like images developing on a sheet of photo-printing paper, and moved towards them. Darden and he tensed and aimed their rifles at the lead figures.

In a voice that was less than a speaking voice, but more than a whisper, MacKenzie challenged the advancing figures. The password was given in a hoarse whisper. It was Sgt. Hoskins and a reconnaissance patrol.

"Advance friend and be recognized," said MacKenzie, and an infantry patrol walked quickly by the foxholes and into the battalion's perimeter. The sergeant leading it and MacKenzie and Darden waved a hand of recognition to each other as the patrol moved almost silently into the perimeter.

MacKenzie and the other men understood their superiors wanted to know where the enemy was and needed patrols to find out. Even so, they felt uneasy outside their own line, at night, because that was when the NKPA found it safest to move. They knew they could meet an enemy patrol, or be ambushed by one. An ambush would be bad, and if they met an NKPA patrol unexpectedly, they knew that could be messy business too. Ambushes are bad for the soldiers ambushed, and meeting actions are messy for both sides.

"Now that you're up, you can take over," whispered MacKenzie to Darden, who nodded in agreement. MacKenzie then sank to the bottom of the foxhole, sat with his legs against his chest, and covered himself with the blanket.

In this battalion, there was no formal guard posting and relief. At all times, since Inchon, the men that had guard duty were in two-man foxholes. Half were on guard, while the other half slept. When the man on guard became too tired to remain alert, he awakened the other man, who then took over while the first man slept. At all times, silence was maintained. The only part of the body of the wakeful man that showed above the foxhole was his head, and he turned it very slowly to scan the area in his fire field for any movement.

Darkness cloaked each man in the valley and hid his exact whereabouts when he was still. Movement could betray where a man was. It invited any nearby enemy to shoot at the vague image that moved.

In the morning, MacKenzie and Darden headed for the field kitchen for a hot breakfast. On the way, Darden said, "I heard yesterday that the ROK II Corps was moving up a few days ago, over to our west, when they were surprised and badly beaten by huge units of Chinks. The story has it that the ROK units on our eastern flank were also savaged and ain't fit to fight no more. I heard some of the attackers were captured and turned out to be Chinese, from several different Chinese armies that are somewhere north of us."

"I heard the same rumors," MacKenzie said, "but I don't like to repeat them. If they're true, we will know soon enough. Repeating bad rumors can spook everyone, and the rumors may be false. We have heard hundreds of rumors since we landed in Korea, and most have been false.

"You remember when you first hunted deer?"

"I sure do," said Darden. "I was probably ten years old when my dad and I went up to my uncle's old plantation. The only things harvested there now are trees and, in hunting season, some fine deer and turkeys."

"You probably had the same experience I had when I first hunted deer. I was a teenager then, and I remember how I would be still for a long time and listen carefully. And after a while, I would think I heard a deer moving near me. You know seasoned hunters call that 'being spooked'. It took a couple of seasons before I learned to tell the sounds of deer moving from the sounds leaves make when a breeze rustles them, and the sounds tree limbs and bushes make when they rub together, and especially the sound of my own blood pumping through my body."

"I know what you mean," said Darden.

"It's the same with us here," said MacKenzie. "Every story someone tells spooks us, because we are not used to this kind of hunting. I hope we're not here for long enough to be able to tell which stories are true and which are rumors, but I discount everything I hear by at least 50 percent."

"That's probably a good thing to do," Darden said, "but even if only half of what I heard is true, there is something big ahead of us. I heard the Chinese advanced somewhere under smoke screens they made by burning the forests they came through. That way they were able to prevent our air reconnaissance from spotting them. I also heard they savaged elements of the (US) 1st Cavalry Division as our units moved northward through the disintegrating ROK units to attack them.

"Our platoon sergeant told me the first sergeant of Company B told him the ROKs collapsed overnight and left their guns, vehicles, and equipment behind when they ran. He said that if that's really what happened, there is a huge empty gap between the Eighth Army and the Tenth Corps yonder on the eastern coast.

"There's another rumor flyin' 'round that the ROK unit, the one that was on our eastern flank, had taken a lot of prisoners during a period of several days, and when the prisoners were interrogated, it turned out each of them was from a different Chinese field army.

"What I heard about the Chinks makes it sound as if they are like the North Koreans multiplied by 10,000. The word is they attacked in hordes: in waves of human infantry in close formation, so no one could fire fast enough to kill all of 'em, and the Chinese that survived the ROK fire finally swept over the South Koreans and destroyed 'most everyone in every unit they attacked.

"The Chinese seem to be even more expert than the North Koreans at regiment-sized infiltration, flanking, and surprise. They position themselves well and try t' shock, surprise, and outflank. I heard they're lightly armed and have no armor and not much artillery. What they have is rifles, light mortars, rocket propelled grenades (RPGs), and hundreds of thousands of soldiers that are die-hard communists and America-haters that are willing to run into machine gun and cannon fire on command. Their infiltration tactics are good soldiering, and their massed attacks are probably the only way they can direct enough firepower at us to try to overcome the great firepower we have."

"I heard similar rumors," said MacKenzie. "By tomorrow, the rumors will either say the Chinese have dropped an atom bomb on our lines, or we may find out they are really there in force, or really not there in force. But the similarity of what I heard today, from different sources, is unusual for a rumor. I hear wide variations of what happened, but enough similarity to make me wonder if there is not some terrible truth underlying those rumors."

Darden was silent as they walked the next few steps towards the field kitchen. Then he said, "Why did Truman send us to Korea? Until the North Koreans invaded the South, I never heard mention of this place. When we were ordered here, some of the men went to the base library and looked in an atlas to see where Korea is."

"I don't know the answer for sure," said MacKenzie, "but I wonder if we are here because Truman was afraid not to send US troops to stop the North Koreans."

"How's that?"

"Do you remember how the right-wing Republicans called the Democrats pinks, and fellow travelers, and commies, and blamed them for the fall of China to the Communists two years after World War II ended?"

"I do. I think their head man is Sen. Taft of Ohio."

"Right. Well, it seems possible that Truman was afraid he would be called an appeaser if he did not act tough when South Korea was invaded. Because of the way the Republicans carried on about China and blamed the Democrats for Communist China's success,

Truman didn't dare to let the North Korean Communists take South Korea. He had to look tough and fight back."

"You mean," Darden said, "he had to talk tough and send us to fight back with outdated weapons."

"Well, yes, but you know what I mean."

"All too well. But do you really reckon that was the whole reason?"

Now Darden waited for an answer from MacKenzie.

"Maybe and maybe not, MacKenzie said. "There is one view that says the Soviets wanted to draw us into a war here, so they could attack and overrun Western Europe. But that has not happened, and it's the Chinese that seem to reckon they have a vital interest in helping North Korea.

"The only other explanation I have read is that Truman and his advisors reckoned the attack happened because the Soviets were trying to see if we would defend against an attack on a country we had said was of no value to us. That explanation makes no sense, unless I add in the theory about Taft and the Republicans, and that Truman feared being blamed for a communist take-over of another country."

"A lot of bad thinking and damned sad reasons to send us here," said Darden.

"True, but don't fret it," MacKenzie said. "If we're being told the truth, the big fight was over and done with after we landed at Inchon and took Seoul. There were only a few nasty skirmishes right after the landing, but no big battles, and we've seen no enemy for several days. The North Korean forces have been routed, and those that are left are on their way to China. We heard South Korean troops reached the Yalu on October 25, and it's now up to us to keep moving northward to create a UN line along the Yalu and capture any North Koreans that have not crossed into China. Dougout Doug says the war will be over in a few more weeks."

"Sure," said Darden, "but the truth you mention doesn't match the steady flow of contrary information we're getting about what is happening north of us."

When they reached the field kitchen, they met Boomer Keefe, a platoon sergeant from Company A. "Heard anything more about Chinese forces?" MacKenzie asked.

"Nothing new," Keefe said. "Probably just the same rumors you all have heard just enlarged in the telling. But it seems to me there must be some truth in them. Our battalion CO (commanding officer) thinks so too and has a duty officer and communications man on duty all night long, every night, and so does each company. If you all look, you all will see every crew-served weapon has been positioned and sighted to fire on the perimeter and their crews are right by them, with extra ammo in place. Those were the battalion commander's orders. He wants to be ready for any truth there may be in the rumors."

After he was ready for the day's movement, MacKenzie sought out his platoon's senior non-commissioned officer, Platoon Sergeant Andrew Smith. MacKenzie had found Smith to be calm and even tempered, even in situations that made other men lose their composure. Here in Korea, amidst the tension generated by combat on the way to the Pusan Perimeter and then during battles to hold it and now amidst continual rumors and heightened alertness, Smith's easygoing disposition and intelligent conversation made him preferred company for MacKenzie.

The two men were products of different parts of Appalachia. Smith was from hills where subsistence farming was supplemented by animal husbandry, including pigs that ran free in nearby woodland, and by hunting and fishing. Cash came from meager sales of produce and meat, including deer meat and hides, as well as from any paid work that could be found. MacKenzie hailed from where the Appalachian foothills blend into gently rolling land on which farming was somewhat profitable; hunting and fishing were usually done for recreation; and paid work was usually available.

Smith, at 6 feet 2 inches tall and 195 pounds, was the larger of the two. He had light blond hair, medium features, and blue eyes. MacKenzie was 6 feet tall and weighed 175 pounds. He had smaller features, reddish hair, and grey eyes. Both had broad cheekbones and shoulders. They were each solidly built and in very good condition.

What the two shared more than geographical kinship was a better knowledge of their world than most of the men with whom they served. Each also had a mind accustomed to seek new information, to question it, reject what made no sense, and to continually re-shape his world view, on the basis of the new information he accepted and absorbed.

3

LOOKING BACK

MacKenzie had met Smith socially shortly after MacKenzie arrived in Japan earlier that year. The two were on a sightseeing excursion to a Japanese shrine and hot springs resort. MacKenzie had sat next to the sergeant on the chartered bus, and the men had become acquainted through the usual small talk.

Darden would normally have ridden next to MacKenzie, but it was right after pay day and Darden had decided to stay in the barracks and shoot craps instead of sightseeing.

"Where you from, Sarge?" MacKenzie asked Smith.

"I was born and bred in northeastern Tennessee, not too far from the Virginia border."

"That must have been hard. I've heard that's a right poor place to earn a living."

"I reckon it is," Smith said. "That's why I was born there. My parents moved there from southern, middle Tennessee as newlyweds, right after they finished teacher training. They had a missionary-like hope they could contribute to improving the educational level there and dedicated their lives to doing that. I remember how happy they were about each of their students who finished high school, and thrilled about the ones that went on to vocational training or college.

"I was born to them relatively late in their lives, after they had taught school for many years: kind of a surprise for them. So, they were fairly old when I finished high school, in 1942, right as the US was really moving ahead fighting the war in North Africa, Europe, and the Pacific. I turned 18 that summer and joined the army. My parents would have preferred for me to go on to college. I had the grades needed to get into a good college, and that would have given me a temporary draft exemption, but with the war on, they understood I felt I had to go.

"They died a few years after that war, and left me with many fine memories of them. They achieved as much as any two people could, while they lived. The real problem with where I grew up is that there are very few jobs and even fewer that enable a man to marry and provide for a wife and a couple of kids. If a man does not have a job in a pulp or lumber mill, he will have a hard time to make a living he can raise a family on. The economics of the area have probably not changed much in sixty years.

"My wife Nancy was in my class in high school. She and I married in 1942, when I was on leave after completing my training. We had two happy weeks together, and then I did not see here again until early in 1946. By that time, we had a fine, four-year-old son.

"I got out of the army briefly, but could not find a job that would enable me to support a family, so I decided to go back into the army. That army's size was being cut then, and I was lucky to get back in with my three stripes intact. Our second child was born in a hospital on an army post, in Missouri, and our third in a post hospital in Georgia."

Smith pulled his wallet from a pocket and took a photo from it. "There she is, with the children. The one she holds was born early this year."

"You certainly have a right pretty wife and fine looking children," MacKenzie said, after studying the photo for a moment.

MacKenzie pointed to the baseball uniform on the eldest of Smith's two sons and said, "Is he on the school team?"

"He sure is. Plays second base and plays it right well. I hope to see him play some time soon.

"The peace-time army moved me twice to different posts, and the family moved along with me. My wife did not like family life at or near army bases, or moving our home. I had to agree with her that it is a kind of rootless way for children to grow up.

"When I was ordered to a Japanese billet, she convinced me it was time for her to take the children and head back to Tennessee and Misty Falls. That's our hometown. That way the children will go to the same schools and make friends that will be their neighbors later in life. They'll have a hometown that they'll be parts of.

"Of course, not having their daddy with them now is not too good for them. Nancy said it's not enough to support them with money and be just a photo on the mantle. She said it will be better, if I can find a job there and avoid dragging them around from base to base or being absent most of the time. I had to agree. Once I did that, it was only a short hop to deciding I will leave the army when this enlistment ends and head home to be with them again.

"Nancy's quite a woman. She already had gotten the hardware store owner to promise me a job when I come home. I can't argue with her about the army. She's too pretty to rile, and I love her too much to want to do that. And how can I argue with a woman that can find me a good job before I'm even there to take it.

"Since Nancy found me that clerk's job," Smith continued, "a neighbor that watched me grow up, and who is now head man in county politics, promised her to get me a job with the highway department when I come home. It won't be the finest job, but will be a few cuts above the hardware store position in pay and even comes with health insurance and some other benefits. It will give me time to settle in and look around."

"Where are you from?" Smith asked MacKenzie.

"Pinckneyville, Georgia," said MacKenzie. "I grew up on the gently rolling woodland edge of the Appalachian foothills. The place is named Pinckneyville, but it's just a farming area and place name on the county map, as well as the name of voter precincts."

"Where's it near?"

"It's near Norcross. That's in Gwinnett County, which is two counties northeast of Atlanta and the next county south of the one

Gainesville is in, but most of our business dealings were in nearby Norcross. We never went to Atlanta and only went to Gainesville for very special purposes."

"Is your daddy a farmer?"

"Nope. He had his own car, light truck, and farm equipment repair shop. Worked as a mechanic, with a little machinist and blacksmith work whenever he needed a part he could not get to repair some farmer's ancient harrow, or other old equipment. His kin have been in the area since the early 1800s and in Georgia for a lot longer. My mother's kin came from western North Carolina sometime after Lincoln's war.

"I spent most of my free time when growing up swimming and fishing in the Chattahoochee, which is only a few miles from our home. I went to nearby schools, helped in my daddy's workshop, hunted small game and fowl, and did a lot of dove shooting. Each fall we hunted deer and doves. In my teens, I pitched for Pinckneyville's amateur baseball team. I also played varsity baseball at Oglethorpe University, which is why I can heave a grenade so well."

"You know, I never heard of Pinckneyville, or Oglethorpe," said Smith. "I know there are an almost endless number of places, but I did not realize there are so many colleges and universities. There must be lebenty-leben thousand colleges in the US, 'cause every few weeks I hear about another I did not know existed. Were your teams good?"

"Well, I should explain that the Pinckneyville team played in the Dixie Youth League, which is a local baseball league. We had no connection with a school. The players all lived in the area, and the team and league were all amateurs and practiced one weekday afternoon a week and played on Saturdays.

"As far as good goes, I can easily tell you how good we were. When we began, we called ourselves the Pinckneyville Sluggers. We had no uniforms. We each wore a white T-shirt and old trousers, and we each had spikes and a mitt.

"During our first season, we played poorly. Some of our friends and neighbors, who were always there to watch us play when we played at our home field, began to advise us that we were really like possums and not sluggers. They said that was true, because when we played at home we looked dead, and when we went on the road we were killed."

Smith laughed, and MacKenzie continued. "By the time we ordered uniform shirts, for the next season, the name Possums seemed kind of natural to us, and we associated the name with Pogo, the cute little cartoon possum a man named Walt Kelly draws for newspapers' comic pages.

"We decided to use the name Possums, and we had a good time with it. If Mr. Kelly knew we also used his little Pogo Possum cartoon character as our emblem, we might have owed money to him, or to the company that sells his cartoon strips to newspapers. But no one outside of our league probably ever heard of us, and we had fun with the name, the Pogo Possum cartoon character, and baseball.

"After we called ourselves the Possums, we must have begun to lighten up and play for the sheer enjoyment of the game, because we knew no one expected any great performances from us any more. Then we began to play better and to coordinate our play with real teamwork. We won a few games and came close a lot more often, and we began to think we could do better. Within two seasons, we were near the top of the league, and the next year we finished second. By that time, the teams we played no longer thought we, or our team name, were funny."

"What about Oglethorpe?" asked Smith.

"Oglethorpe lies in the county that is mostly between Gwinnett County and the county Atlanta is in. I played for its baseball team while I was there and enjoyed playing for it. I would be playing there yet, but I was graduated with a B.A. degree and thereby became ineligible to play for the school any longer."

"Did you pitch for Oglethorpe?"

"Yup. I pitched for Oglethorpe the same as I did for Pinckneyville."

"Was Oglethorpe's team any good?"

"We were pretty good. Especially considering that the baseball scholarships did not amount to much. We were an academic school and played teams that were mostly the same."

"Isn't MacKenzie a Scotch name?" asked Smith.

"Yup, it's Scots, and my daddy has records of his family in Georgia that go back to the time shortly after the colony was founded. His people spoke Gaelic when they came and apparently bought books and other kinds of written material in their language from North Carolina, where there was a larger settlement that used the Gaelic. Within two generations, his forebears moved on from the eastern coast into many other parts of the nation's westward expansion.

"Somehow, my daddy's forebears kept spelling the family's name 'Mac', when most others of their background began to spell it

'Mc'. I understand MacKenzie means son of Kenzie, or kin of Kenzie. I reckon Kenzie must have been an important chief back in early historic times, or during the folk-story time before that, but don't know a thing about him. What about you? You ever play for a baseball team?"

"I never played for a baseball team, but I was a lineman, a left tackle, on the county high school's football team, and when not in school, or playing football, sure did enjoy hunting and fishing."

"Names are interesting," said Smith. "I reckon there is often something in a name that can affect self-evaluation and self-esteem in unexpected ways. My parents named me Andrew, after my daddy's daddy, and Forrest after General Nathan Bedford Forrest, the great Confederate general. My parents held him to be a great example of what a good man will do if given an opportunity.

"You know, Forrest was born in the backwoods to a pioneer family and never had any formal education. At age 14, his daddy died and he had to fend for his mother and a parcel of younger brothers and sisters. He eventually prospered as a slave and horse trader and later as a Mississippi planter."

"Yup, I agree names can be important to a person, and I reckon Forrest was a man that was especially brilliant and had a strong, good character."

"Why, Forrest was so effective in battle tactics and overall strategy that US Gen. Sherman said Forrest had to be captured or killed, even if the US lost 10,000 soldiers dead to do it and it bankrupted the US treasury in the process. I reckon Forrest was the finest military genius yet grown in the Western Hemisphere."

"You're preaching to the choir," said MacKenzie. "We know about him in Georgia. He once led his men on a seemingly impossible ride and prevented the US Army from destroying the munitions factories and other factories around Rome, Georgia, and the railroads in northern Georgia. He was a great leader.

"It's too bad what happened then is not taught in schools any more. It's not possible now to talk about those times without having to explain a huge amount of history, so a listener can understand the situation in which events happened."

"You're right," said Smith. "But that's government policy. They can't portray Lincoln as a hero unless they portray our side as evil."

The conversation paused. When it resumed, Smith said, "You know, Mac, during the last war and this one, I have known hundreds of men, and do you know, I never yet met a man whose daddy was a US senator or congressman. And I never met anyone in a combat unit that knew someone that knew a US senator's or congressman's son either. Once I'm out, I plan to write letters to my senators and congressmen and tell them to see to it that their sons and the sons of other rich and privileged people do their part for the country that protects their wealth. I reckon I'll send copies of those letters to newspapers too.

"Mac, you're a college man. How did you come to be here as a common dog face."

MacKenzie hesitated for a moment and then said, "Well, after I earned that Bachelor of Arts degree, I decided started to earn a post-graduate degree, but dropped out. That made me eligible for the draft. Once the draft board learned I would no longer be a student, it was only a matter of two months before I was drafted. I was in for more than half a year, when I was shipped here to Japan. This is a good duty station, and I've seen a lot I never would have seen if the army had not sent me here. There's not much better duty to be had."

"That's true. It is good and easy. Not like the troops in Western Europe, where they are always training and combat ready."

"You have brothers and sisters?"

"I had two older brothers. My brother Harold, the eldest, enlisted in the marines, right after Pearl Harbor. He died in 1945, during the battle for Okinawa. William, my other brother, enlisted in the army and fought through the South Pacific campaigns MacArthur commanded. He ended nearly three years of combat in the battle for Manila, in the Philippines.

"He came home with several medals for heroism and seemed to settle back into a quieter life. But after a while, it became clear he was not really at ease in the quiet world of Pinckneyville. He seemed always to be a bit unhappy or serious and would take long walks, or camp alone, in the hills near the Tennessee line. Sometimes, when he was asleep, we could hear him talking or shouting. He slept restlessly, and his mind seemed to be back in a skirmish or battle he had been in.

"Even so, he got on with daily life and adjusted enough on the surface, for he got a job and became engaged to marry a really sweet woman he had gone to high school with. We thought he was settling in again. None of us understood he was not just unhappy. He was deeply depressed.

"One Sunday morning he was nowhere to be found. We were ready to go to church together and his fiancée and he were supposed to talk with the minister after the service about the wedding, which was only two months away. We finally gave up waiting and went to church without him.

"When we came home, the hounds were upset. They had been baying and fussing before we left, but we had had no time then to bother with them. We had left them outside, where we always left them when we went to church. When we came home, dad called them to come in, but instead of coming when he called them, they stayed by a shed in a field behind the house, and whined and bayed and moved around near the shed. They wouldn't come no matter how he called, and that was unusual, for they were fine hunting hounds and always obedient.

"Finally, my dad walked across the field and back behind the shed to see what they were so agitated about and found Bill's corpse. Bill had sat down with his back against a tree, put a shotgun into his mouth, and pulled the trigger. Thunder storms had passed over the area the night before and early that morning, and the shot fired behind the shed had gone unnoticed.

"I mean to tell you we were upset. The shock of Bill's death seemed to take a lot of life out of my folks. My daddy died almost a year later, and mom passed on only a few months after him. They were in their fifties and had seemed to be healthy. Then both died of nothing a medical doctor could identify. They apparently lost their will to live, and died.

"Some psychologists say now that men like Bill should be given extensive psychological counseling by the US government, before or after they are discharged from the military and returned to civilian life. The military takes men from non-violent homes and neighborhoods,

25

and trains them to kill, and rewards those that kill efficiently. Those men learn to shut out everything they have been taught at home, in Sunday school, and in civil society. They become expert at inflicting death and injury on demonized enemies.

"Then the military's need for them ends and their killing skills are no longer needed. They are then turned out of the military and back to a quiet, mild world that punishes injuring and killing and does not relate to their violent experiences or understand their emotional turmoil and pain.

"Most of those men manage to re-open the compartment in which they had closed their learning from childhood and church, and to compartmentalize and close off what the military taught them and what they did because of their military training.

"But some can't close off and forget what they did in the military. What they did stays with them and haunts them, particularly when they try to rest. That's when the dead crawl at them and they kill again and again."

At that moment, the bus rolled into the parking place near the shrine, and Smith, MacKenzie, and the other passengers stepped off to take a guided tour.

4

MESSAGES

"Happy Thanksgiving," said Smith, as he joined a group of men from his platoon.

"Mind if I pull up a cold stone to sit on and join you in this feast?"

"There's plenty of cold stone to go around," one soldier said, "and enough of this here chow the army flew in from Japan to serve everyone twice. They must have landed this food at Pusan or Inchon and carried it here by truck. What a lot of work for one meal."

"Knock it off," another man said. "They just wanted us to have the best they can give us. I appreciate it."

"What an expense," said another man.

"I don't mind the expense," contributed the man next to him. "I'm worth it. I think this is great. They ought to feed us like this every day."

"The best they can give me is a one-way ticket back to the States, but I'll settle for Japan," was the answer. "I'll buy my own food when they do."

"I'd appreciate it more if they supplied us with spare parts for the vehicles," said another man.

"Yeah, no spare parts for any vehicles," said another man. "Just heaps of empty aluminum containers and wooden crates around us from everything that goes with Thanksgiving dinner. We can get by with rations and do without this extravagance, but we can't chase the Commies without our vehicles. Someone in Tokyo or DC has screwed up thinking."

The food served them included turkey, gravy, cranberry sauce, asparagus, tomatoes, shrimp cocktail, and fruit cake or pumpkin pie, or mince pie.

The cold was intense, and the men were crouched, for warmth around a fire made from wood from crates that had held some of the food they ate. The food was piping hot when served at a chow line by the nearby field kitchen, but the gravy was cool by the time they sat to eat. Only the turkey meat held warmth for a couple of minutes. Anything not eaten quickly froze.

"Where'd you get the skillet?" said one soldier, when he noticed the skillet another had pulled from his pack and put onto the fire to warm his food, some of which was now cold.

"Carried it with me from Japan. Never can tell when it might be handy. I used it a few days ago to fry eggs."

"Where'd you get fresh eggs?"

"Traded them from an old woman. Gave her a worn shirt and she gave me two eggs. Good deal for both of us!"

A rifleman in a group behind them was playing "My Old Kentucky Home" on a harmonica, and the men around him had begun to sing to the tune. The player was Johnson, a young man from some place in eastern Kentucky whose wife had sent him a photo of their son, who had been born only two weeks earlier. Johnson had been around to almost everyone in the company since he got the photo, to show it. He was so proud of the little, wrinkled, pink creature in the photo that his happiness had proven a bit contagious.

A soldier named Bodmer, from Illinois, looked up and, ignoring the chatter, looked at the men around the campfire and said, "There have been a few reported sightings of Chinese troops, though I've not heard that any shots have been fired by them. But there are some Chinese soldiers out there watching us and waiting."

"Hell, soldier, don't sweat it. Dougout Doug says we'll be home by Christmas," said a rifleman across from him. "The unit just south of us has begun to clean its equipment and pack everything surplus, for shipment back to the States."

"Yup," said Darden, "the commanding officer of our 1st Battalion had his men to turn in their helmets, so they can be painted and look good when the men get back to Japan. The whole battalion has only helmet liners on, until the re-painted tin hats come back."

"I hope they're not overly optimistic," said MacKenzie. "There are a few reasons that make me think they might be sorely disappointed."

"I reckon what happens next depends upon what Dougout Doug decides to have us do next," said Smith. "I reckon it's probable there are Chinese watching us, and they're not hanging around in this freezing weather for their health. I reckon they are waiting to see what we do. If we are ordered to stop here and create a defensive line, they may do nothing. But if we keep on heading for the Yalu, unless I'm very mistaken, we're in for a heap of fighting."

"What do you mean?" asked Kutscher, a man from northern California, who looked at Bodmer with his brow deeply furrowed with worry wrinkles. "You mean they will attack again, if we move northward?"

"That's just what I mean," said Smith. "You know what they did to almost every UN unit they attacked, just a few weeks ago. I reckon that was just a foretaste of what they plan to try to do to us, if we continue towards the Yalu. They attacked in strength, smashed most UN units they attacked, and then broke off the battles, when they could have continued.

"If we head for the Yalu again and they attack again, I don't reckon they will break off again. That river is part of their border, and they probably do not want us there any more than we would want a very large, well-armed, hostile, foreign army to advance to one of our borders."

The man who had asked the question looked at his mess plate and shoved at the now cold food on it a little. Then he said, "I hope you're wrong, Sergeant."

Bodmer nodded swift agreement with that sentiment.

"I hope I'm wrong too," said Smith. "If the Chinese are in this war, the whole shooting match has begun over again, and then discharges will be as frozen as they are now. But I can only guess why they attacked, beat, or bloodied every unit they attacked and then disappeared. I hope this isn't the beginning of another war. We don't have the manpower to fight the Chinese on their own border.

"If we advance northward, I will want you all to be alert for a possible enemy attack, or for any of their scouting parties you all might spot. You all can bet they will be there, watching around our front, flanks, and maybe even in the rear. We'll do a lot better if we are always ready for an attack and try our best to know where they are."

Bodmer said, "I can't think of any reason the Chinese are here, except to help to stop us. I hope I'm wrong, because it will be mighty messy if we get into a war with the Chinese."

Smith kicked at the frozen ground by his right toe and said, "I reckon I've fought enough, what with World War II and the North Koreans. I've fought in two wars now, and they're enough for me. I don't want to have to fight a third war against the Chinese."

A corporal named DeLancy, from Alabama, said, "I'm not really sure why Korea is important enough for us to fight over. We had no military presence here until after North Korea invaded, and our government had even said Korea was outside our security area. Then it rousts us out of our lush occupation duty in Japan, and tells us to go stop tanks using outdated, ineffective anti-tank weapons, and inadequate mines. That sudden about face confuses me. Why did it happen?"

Bates, a soldier from Arkansas, said, "I don't care why they sent us here. All I care about is that this war ends soon. I don't want to climb another hill. I clum enough here to last me for a lifetime."

That night the temperature plunged far below freezing, and the GIs' main interest was to stay warm enough to survive the night. Except for the men on duty in shallow foxholes around the battalion's perimeter, the GIs slept on the flat, frozen ground, their blankets thrown over them, and usually clustered against each other for warmth. Sleep was fitful, and safely so, for if a man slept too soundly, he could suffer frost bitten fingers, toes, and even feet.

Almost each day now someone was sent back to a field hospital with blackened fingers, toes, or feet that would have to be cut off, and others were sent back with lesser stages of frostbite.

Freezing weather carried with it only one benefit for the GIs. Before it, Korea was the smell of human excrement used to fertilize rice paddies and the smell of kimchi, a favorite Korean food made of cabbage and garlic. The excrement and kimchi smells blended together and heightened each other. They assaulted the newcomer to Korea the moment he stepped onto a transport's gangplank, on his way from ship to dock. When winter's savage talons seized the land and paddies froze, GIs noticed Korea's pre-freeze-excrement smell disappeared, and the kimchi smell became less terrible.

Early the next morning, November 25, 1950, the day after US military field units in Korea celebrated US Thanksgiving Day, the men of Smith's platoon were wakened by the familiar sound of, "Rise and shine, everybody up and ready to move out by 0730 hours."

Smith's voice was only loud enough to effectively break through the light sleep most of the men slept. He spoke his orders to the men of the platoon as he walked through the area where they lay asleep.

"Everyone up and be ready to move out by 0730 hours," he repeated. "We have orders to move northward to the Yalu. Thanksgiving was yesterday. Today we are soldiers again, not guests at a dinner."

"Oh, shit! To the Yalu!" said a soldier next to MacKenzie.

MacKenzie just half sucked in his lower lip and shook his head slightly from side to side.

Once ready to move, the men of the battalion boarded trucks and the battalion's vehicle train moved northward, following the twisting valley road.

The battalion moved several miles along the narrow, dirt road, churning up a dust cloud around it, its engines sending out a loud, clear message on all sides that they were approaching.

A rest stop was ordered after several hours, and the men piled out of the vehicles to eat C rations and relax. The air was cold and the temperature freezing, but more bearable now that the sun was up. Their summer uniforms offered no protection from the Siberian winter that had begun to snarl warnings it was on its way in full force.

Several groups of men hacked apart trees and bushes and built fires with the wood and brush they gathered from the sparse vegetation on the lower slopes of the hills on each side of the road. Their empty C ration containers were left by the roadside.

After the rest stop, the infantrymen again boarded the company's 2-1/2-ton trucks, jeeps, and armor, and the battalion moved northward again. By late afternoon, they had reached a place where the road narrowed and dipped slightly through a 100-yard-wide gap and into a valley that had high, steep ridges on each side. After all the battalion's vehicles had passed through the gap and into the valley, Chinese troops dug in on the gap's western side began to rake the vehicles with rifle and machine gun fire. Mortar rounds fell near the crowded vehicles but had little effect at first. The first Chinese mortar rounds did not hit any vehicles.

The unexpected attack caused temporary chaos in the battalion, and men and officers hustled off the trucks and jeeps and dived behind and under vehicles for protection. Other officers quickly ordered the men to return fire.

An M-19 anti-aircraft vehicle was driven forward, and its gunner began to rake the slope on the western side of the gap with the vehicle's twin-mounted, 40-mm canons while the tanks added their fire. The driver of the lead tank, a thin-skinned Chaffee, tried to re-position it, so its gunner could fire at the attackers' positions. However, in that part of the narrow valley, the ridge's crest, where some enemy troops were dug in, was too high for the Chaffee's gunner to be able to raise the 75-mm gun high enough to aim direct, effective fire onto the uppermost Chinese positions.

Behind the Chaffee, several trucks and jeeps were in flames, blocking the road. A Sherman tank moved back along the column and shoved the burning vehicles off the dirt road onto its narrow shoulder. It then moved ahead to where it could fire its 76-mm main gun, when it sighted targets. When it rolled near MacKenzie and fired its main gun, there was a bright flash; the ground shook; and sudden, tremendous air pressure compressed his lungs each time. As the tank's driver continued to reposition the vehicle, only the tank's turret-mounted 50-cal. machine gun was fired at the enemy, but without good effect.

The Chinese began to find their targets more effectively and raked the column with machine gun, rifle, and mortar fire. As mortar rounds exploded around them, GIs moved swiftly to the rear of the vehicles and tanks.

The battalion's light mortars had been set up quickly and began to fire at suspected enemy positions. Explosions and cascades of steel on the hillside quickly followed the whoosh-like sound of mortar rounds leaving mortar tubes. The rounds crashed amongst trees, bushes, and stony slopes along the gap, and the noise rose to a deafening level, while smoke from explosions and gun and small arms fire created a cloud on the valley's floor, around US positions.

Heavy weapons were also set up, including twelve 50-cal. machine guns. When probable Chinese positions were identified, these were fired at them.

The tank cannons and anti-aircraft guns crisscrossed a larger area than that from which the enemy's fire came and, along with mortar rounds, flung stone, wood, and steel into the air, along with clouds of dirt as the rounds blew holes in the hill's surface and cut apart any enemy unfortunate enough to be near where they hit. Smoke from the cannon and anti-aircraft rounds added to the smoke and dust layer that rose from the valley floor and made it hard to see 200 feet ahead.

The effect of the US fire concentrated on the hillside was to blow trees and bushes apart and shoot particles of stone and dirt skywards along with metal fragments. These bounced off hard surfaces and imbedded themselves in soft ones.

The noise of all those weapons shooting and rounds exploding caused the ground to vibrate, while canon fire compressed the lungs of those nearby and caused continual ringing in the ears. The noise level rose and ears hurt and heads seemed to ring, as rapid and violent air vibrations assaulted the eardrums and momentarily blocked other sounds from being heard. Arm motions were needed to ensure that shouted commands were understood.

The men of Company B hunkered down behind trucks and tanks. After the battalion's armor, mortars, and machine guns had fired on the lower hillside for close to twenty minutes, Lt. Col. McClusky, the battalion commander, ordered their fire confined to the hill's middle elevation and Company B's 1st, 2nd, and 3rd platoons to move up the slopes to find and destroy all resistance. The company's 4th platoon was held in reserve.

When the attack began, the battalion's vehicles had been strung out along more than a mile of road. After two hours of intense fighting and slow progress in moving up the slopes and northward through the long valley, Col. McClusky radioed regiment that he wanted to reverse course and withdraw southward and out of the valley. Darkness would come by mid-afternoon, and burning vehicles would enable the

Crew members of a 75-mm recoilless rifle, and GIs nearby, hold their
ears to try to protect their hearing from the blast, as the weapon
fires. Heavy weapons, artillery, and even concentrated small-arms
fire injured the hearing of men nearby.

U.S. Army photo

enemy to continue to fire down onto the column through the smoke and dust with some degree of accuracy. The thought of a night-time attack by the enemy against GIs not protected by perimeter defenses was active in the colonel's thoughts. He knew it was probable.

If his command moved ahead, it would be farther from the regiment's other battalions and could not protect itself anywhere in the narrow valley from an enemy that could fire down on it. Total annihilation of his command could result from that. The battalion remained an effective fighting unit, and he wanted to get his men away from the ambush before it became dark and to a place where it could defend itself. At 1400 hours, he received word to withdraw and attack the gap at dawn tomorrow.

Company B was ordered back to the valley floor and to walk along by the vehicles as the battalion withdrew. Both sides continued to fire while it retraced its march of earlier that day. Tracers from Chinese and US machine guns drew momentarily moving arcs of light from the hills to the valley and back again. The only steady light was from burning vehicles.

The intact vehicles were turned to face southward and the wounded and dead loaded on to the trucks. The infantrymen stayed alongside vehicles and fired at muzzle flashes on the hills. The battalion's machine gun crews and light mortars were kept in action as the battalion positioned itself to withdraw. Company B was initially with them to try to ensure they would be able to board trucks and follow the rest of the battalion.

MacKenzie fired at a point on the nearest slope from which he thought one of the enemy had fired. It was his last round, and he looked at the man next to him to ask if he could spare several clips of ammo. It was only then he noticed that the man and several beyond that man were not firing. Several were bellies down on the dirt and either looking at the fire fight, or kneeling on one knee with their rifles in both hands and staring. Not staring to see if they could help, but staring in shock, awe, and fear.

MacKenzie poked the man next to him and repeated his request in a more command-like tone. The man moved only enough to give several clips of rifle ammo to MacKenzie, who was then able to continue his fight.

MacKenzie wondered why he did not react the same as the GIs by his side who stared in frozen fear or hugged the ground in terror. Combat sharpened his senses even more than hunting game, more than he ever thought was possible. He could feel the difference in his breathing. He knew fear, but it did not immobilize or overwhelm him. He was grateful for that, whatever the reason.

To facilitate the withdrawal, Col. McClusky ordered Company B to move up the southern part of the western hillside to engage the enemy again and distract them while the withdrawal was made. Capt. Wilson, Company B's commander, formed his men by several trucks. The 1st, 2nd, and 4th platoons would be the attacking force, and 3rd Platoon would be in reserve. It would remain on the road until called for.

The company's platoon lieutenants and sergeants moved up and down the roadside and rousted out their men. The officers held a carbine in one hand and a 45-cal. pistol in the other, which they waved at the men as they ordered them up and into action. Most men responded quickly, and the slackers responded too, choosing possible death or injury from the enemy to certain death at a lieutenant or noncom's hand.

Capt. Wilson gave the order for the company to follow him forward, and platoon officers and noncoms led their units forward across the road and up the slope. As they moved onto the slope, the small trees and bushes caused men to become separated from their squads. By the time the company was a few hundred feet up the slope, the leaders had to keep the momentum of the upward attack and also try to re-group their men. Many men were no longer with their own squads and could not see where they should be.

A mortar round exploded ahead of MacKenzie and his squad and several men were blown to each side of the blast and backward by it. Most of the men hunkered down as more mortar rounds exploded ahead of them. Capt. Wilson rose and shouted above the boom and clatter of the battle, "Follow me!" and each platoon commander repeated the order to his squad noncoms and they to their squads. Then Capt. Wilson waved his right arm forward, and the company moved ahead again up the steep hillside.

MacKenzie, followed by his squad, followed his platoon leader. He looked to the nearby spot where another mortar round had exploded and saw it had landed next to several men. One was now a bisected, disemboweled corpse with an arm and part of the head missing. Another corpse was missing the lower legs and had terrible gashes on the torso and face. A third man, ashen grey, writhing and bleeding from shrapnel wounds along his body's left side, lay on his right side, unable to turn onto his back because he was hindered by the irregular terrain and stubble of bushes that had been blasted apart by the explosion that wounded him.

MacKenzie looked fleetingly at the dead and wounded as he continued to move up the slope. He saw the wounded man was from his platoon, but wondered whose dismembered corpses he had just seen? The unattached limbs and mangled, bisected torso were scattered over an area several yards wide. He wondered if one might be Zippolo, a young draftee from Scranton, Pensylvania, but was not certain.

As the platoon climbed upwards, a mortar round fell ahead of MacKenzie and about 30 feet to his left. It fell directly in front of a GI whose helmet was blown off, along with his head. Both helmet and head flew backward downhill separately with the force of projectiles, and the corpse was spun in a backward somersault and fell on its back spewing blood over the hillside and onto men nearby.

MacKenzie's stomach tightened in a knot, his mouth became dry, and he felt a cold and sickly feeling he had not felt since his first combat months ago. Anger quickly replaced fear, and he looked ahead again and led his squad as they climbed with ever greater difficulty up the steep slope. Adrenaline now pumped through his system, and he and his squad advanced up the slope, shooting back at muzzle flashes that sent intended death at them.

It was difficult terrain on which to fight. It was hard for the men to climb and at the same time be alert for enemy troops. The small ravines also made it difficult for officers and noncoms to keep their commands in sight for command and control purposes. Half the fight was to climb the steep slope. The other half was to spot well-concealed Chinese soldiers ahead and on both sides.

As they advanced, there were brief firefights between GIs and Chinese. Men of the 2nd Platoon killed Chinese riflemen with bullets and grenades and destroyed two machine guns and their crews with grenades. As they reached mid-way up the slope, the soldier on MacKenzie's left made a noise as he straightened up and then fell forward on his face, motionless. The man was from MacKenzie's squad. He was one of those who had been frozen by fear and had not fired his rifle when the battalion was pinned down on the road.

The 2nd Platoon neared the mid-way point of the slope, and enemy machine gun fire ripped the earth apart in a line just ahead of them. The machine gun was not easily seen, because it was behind a low stone wall about two feet high, and had a tree branch covering part of it. Several GIs threw fragmentation grenades at the machine gun emplacement, but these fell short by a few feet, and the stone wall protected the Chinese in the gun emplacement from shrapnel.

The fight with the machine gun emplacement ended when a GI who had moved up the hill and to the northern side of the emplacement was able to aim his rifle at the gun crew and kill both crew members and two riflemen who were with them. After that, it took only a few minutes for the platoon to move up above where the machine gun had been.

As MacKenzie continued moving upwards, he thought he saw a weapon fired in his direction. He knelt, aimed at the point where he reckoned the shot came from, and fired three rounds at it. He heard a groan and the sound of something like a rifle falling several feet. When he reached the spot he had fired at, he found a Chinese soldier leaning over a low stone emplacement, in a position that had been scooped out of the hill and surrounded with stones and tree branches. He was motionless, with one arm outstretched and the other on the emplacement. He seemed very dead. In front of the emplacement was a rifle that had fallen from his hands.

MacKenzie reckoned the man was dead, but pushed the body with his rifle butt until he had moved it enough to see a gaping hole just below the skull where a bullet had gone through the neck and blown out flesh and backbone. Several members of MacKenzie's squad watched with only casual interest.

Then MacKenzie looked at his squad, spread out mostly behind him, and motioned them to move ahead with him. They continued up the hill with the rest of the company, in a semblance of a firing line.

When MacKenzie looked again for his squad, he saw they were spread out just behind him. He waved his arm again in a motion that told them to move ahead faster to keep up with him.

As the platoons moved, their line was uneven, and on the right flank, it sloped downwards. Fourth Platoon was new to the company. It was composed almost completely of enlisted draftees and officers and noncoms ordered from desk jobs to a combat unit. This was their first combat experience. It was clear their difficulty was at both the command and obedience levels. MacKenzie saw sergeants motioning men to move upwards towards the enemy, while their men hugged the ground and ignored orders.

MacKenzie thought, "You can't preach love and non-violence from the time a boy is a young child until he is a grown man and expect him to suddenly change and become a competent killer. He has been conditioned one way, and cannot suddenly un-do the indoctrination of his formative years and begin to deliberately kill or maim men he does not know and has never even seen."

He reckoned many of the men had probably never fired a rifle before the army made them do so on a firing range. None had probably ever hunted and killed small game, fowl, or big game. Probably not even a squirrel. They got their meat, wrapped and bloodless, from a grocer's meat counter, and never thought about where the steak or hamburger came from.

As he grasped the stub of a slim tree trunk, which was all that remained of a tree, and hauled himself another few feet up the hillside, he thought, "What kind of society would we have, if the military found an easy way to make peaceful men into efficient killers? What would happen when they returned to society as civilians?

"It would be much easier for most men to be in the air force and press a button and kill people they can not see and whose dismembered and burned corpses they will never see. Crap! Even women can be technically competent killers with the right technology at their disposal."

Capt. Wilson had also seen the way 4th Platoon hung back and moved to remedy it. He left Lt. Lauterbach, the company's next most senior officer, in charge of 1st and 2nd Platoons and moved across the slope and took command of 4th Platoon. With Capt. Wilson's guidance and prodding, 2nd Lt. Collins and 4th Platoon began to move ahead and finally came up almost into the somewhat horizontal line the other platoons were in, as they moved upwards.

The platoons reached the crest of the hill at dusk, just before sudden, winter darkness fell on Korea. There was no twilight, just dusk and then night. The troops ignored the imminent darkness and worked their way southward on the hillside, exchanging fire with enemy soldiers and then advancing over enemy corpses. It was slow going. To help, flares were fired into the darkening sky by a mortar crew on the road.

Only occasionally was it possible to use a grenade to destroy an enemy position, since the GIs were usually at too great a distance from their foe to throw one. Rifles and BARs were used almost exclusively as they advanced.

Smith moved up beside MacKenzie, who was moving ahead with his squad over the stony terrain. He stopped at MacKenzie's side, as MacKenzie and his squad reached a level about 1,000 feet above the road and near a narrow, fairly flat ledge on which were a machine-gun crew and several Chinese soldiers armed with rifles. The machine gun was emplaced so as to be able to sweep the valley when the battalion came within range.

A swift firefight followed, and men dropped on both sides. The Chinese soldier nearest the GIs, who was armed with a pistol, bent his head and armed a percussion grenade he held in one hand. Then he lobbed it over the GIs nearest him so it would drop behind them and ahead of others following them. Smith, about the third GI away from the grenade thrower, jumped high into the air, grabbed the explosive, and then swiftly hurled it towards the Chinese position. The grenade fell into the machine gun emplacement and exploded, knocking the Chinese to the ground.

From the other side of the ridge came the sound of firing and explosions. Then silence.

The men in MacKenzie's squad advanced into the emplacement and ensured no Chinese survived. Smith looked at the Chinese corpses that lay at their feet.

"The same quilted, cotton jackets and cloth shoes that look like tennis shoes," he said, as he looked at the dead Chinese. "Both armies are freezing their asses off here, but their quilted uniforms look warmer than our summer ones."

MacKenzie picked up a pouch that looked differently than the rest of the gear on the ledge and opened it.

"What do you think of this, Sarge," he asked, as he looked at papers he had taken from it. "These certainly do not look like letters from home."

"No, they don't," agreed Smith. "They probably belonged to the soldier that threw the firecracker at us. I reckon he might have been an officer. The pouch and contents should be sent to the battalion commander, so he can find out if it has worthwhile info in it."

At that time, Lt. Lauterbach, half shadow in cloud-veiled moonlight, clattered down from the ridge and joined them. He had been with men that had cleared the ridge's rear area of three mortar emplacements and came to Smith and MacKenzie to ask why they and the men with them had halted.

Smith showed him the pouch's content and the lieutenant looked it over and then put it back into the pouch. He told Smith, "Sergeant, send one man to give this pouch to Capt. Wilson, and tell him I need a man with a radio here pronto. Ours is on the fritz. Tell the captain I plan to continue to advance to the gap and it should be safe then for the battalion to move out of the valley.

Supporting fire for Company B, from heavy weapons and guns on the valley floor, had been available since the company got a third of the way up the hill. Those weapons had been able to fire at the lower slope, but not the mid-level, until they were positioned far enough from those targets to raise their guns to the right angle to send projectiles into the hill's mid and higher elevations.

Two Sherman tanks at the company's tail end fired their 76-mm guns, and two 75-mm pack howitzers, unlimbered and positioned to fire along the slope's upper level, added their fire power to the battle. The fire from tanks, howitzers, machine guns, mortars, and riflemen filled the narrow valley with tremendous noise. Smoke from firing, explosions, bullet and shrapnel impacts drifted down the hillside.

The valley's floor was also covered with a veil of acrid gun smoke and dust. The wind blew across the ridges on each side of the steep-sided valley, at an angle that left the smoke and dust almost undisturbed in the valley. As a result, a blend of dust and smoke hung in the air over the valley's floor, further veiling darkness-obscured US troops moving southward and partly obscuring the lower hillside. The ground shook and the air vibrated strongly and repeatedly, and the valley's high walls held the noise in and make it louder than it should have been.

Darkness gave the battle an added, eerie aspect, as flares and projectiles of various calibers and millimeters streaked through the frigid night air trailing white, yellow, and reddish pink light and then exploded like huge blooms of red, yellow, and white. There were moments when the men and equipment were nearly as visible through the dust and smoke as they would have been in the late afternoon. The brilliantly bright flashes affected the eyes of those on the valley floor and the men there saw thousands of light points even after the firing ended.

Lt. Lauterbach and the 1ˢᵗ Platoon's commander re-deployed their men and moved southward. Only when they were dangerously near an enemy were the GIs able to spot that enemy. Lauterbach, Smith, MacKenzie and several soldiers from MacKenzie's squad crouched behind stone outcrops and looked farther south at what, in a flare's light, seemed to be bunker-like Chinese emplacements part way down the hill. From those positions, the Chinese kept up steady and sometimes accurate fire at GIs and vehicles in the valley.

The GI sent with the message for Capt. Wilson returned, about an hour later, with a soldier carrying a portable radio. They had clawed their way over the darkened hillside, behind the platoon's moving position and reported to Lt. Lauterbach.

The soldier sent to get a portable radio and operator knelt on one knee panting and said, "I'm lucky to be alive. In this darkness, the men of the other platoon did not know if we are GIs or Chinese, and one man shot at me. Lucky for me his aim was off." White puffs of vapor came from his mouth and showed how heavily he breathed. His breath also formed a frosted rim around his mouth as it froze on his beard stubble.

Lt. Lauterbach slapped the upper arm of the dirt-covered, winded soldier to cheer him up and said, "Good man. I'm glad you made it." To the soldier with the radio he said, "Call Capt. Wilson and tell him you are with the 1ˢᵗ and 2ⁿᵈ Platoons. Ask him to relay these coordinates for our positions and these for the Chinese emplacements south of us. Ask him to call for battalion to fire on the Chinese positions."

The radioman called Capt. Wilson and relayed the coordinates. The battalion's mortar crews, in the valley, were soon lobbing rounds over the platoons. Their first rounds dropped onto the hill short of the Chinese, but Lt. Lauterbach was on the radio at once and let them know where the rounds hit. The next rounds exploded only a little short of the Chinese, and the ones after them fell on and around each emplacement, sending stone, wood, dirt, and body parts flying into the air, accompanied by a roar and daylight-bright flash caused by each exploding mortar round.

The explosions were near enough so ground under the platoons shook. The men suspected a round or two from a tank's main gun might also have reached the elevation and helped with the destruction.

Capt. Wilson radioed Lt. Lauterbach to hold his position and, after a short while, joined him. The two talked for several minutes, and then the captain left to lead the 4th platoon to a level below the 1st and 2nd Platoons, where it became the left flank of their advance towards the gap's southern end.

Lt. Lauterbach had the radioman call for fire on the hill's southern end, ahead of Company B's advance. The bombardment began again farther ahead of the GIs. Then, with a sudden bright flash and resounding blast that shook the hill and knocked men to their knees, a Chinese position about 200 yards south and lower on the hill exploded and dirt, wood, stone, steel, and body parts went flying high into the air.

Lt. Lauterbach rose from a crouching position behind a large stone and waved his outstretched arm with hand straight upward, and brought the arm downwards in a motion from his shoulder toward the area ahead of him, and shouted, "Follow me!"

The GIs rose from behind the low ridges and rises they had ducked behind for cover and moved forward and downward toward enemy positions left on the hillside.

The infantrymen advanced and took the hill yard by yard. They encountered only rifle fire. The platoon continued until, nearly four hours after the battle began, they reached the gap's southern end and the valley's floor.

Even when not more than a dozen Chinese soldiers were left and each was completely isolated from the others and there was no hope of victory for them, they had resisted defiantly and as effectively as they could. Their weapons were light compared with the GIs firepower. Concealment, position, and initial surprise were their only allies, but they were determined to win or sell their lives as dearly as they could.

When the last Chinese soldier had been killed, the GIs were ordered back to scour the hillside and help medics to find the seriously wounded and carry them and GIs' corpses to the valley floor.

Forty-two men of Company B had been killed and more than 50 seriously wounded. More than 80 others had been wounded, but remained combat fit. In addition, several GIs on the valley floor had been killed and others wounded. Several trucks and jeeps had been destroyed by mortar and machine-gun fire, and a mortar had disabled the Chaffee, which later burst into flames. The dead GIs' corpses were stacked atop each other in one truck, and the wounded were loaded aboard other trucks.

Capt. Wilson and the platoon commanders shared information about the enemy's strength and estimated that no more than 200 Chinese soldiers had been entrenched on the hillside when the ambush began. That was reported by the captain to Col. McClusky, as well as the fact that every Chinese soldier had died fighting stubbornly and bravely, and none had surrendered.

5

CAMP

After he reviewed the situation with his company commanders, Col. McClusky tried to contact regimental headquarters to report the battle and the battalion's condition and location and ask for further orders. He had been unable to reach regiment during the battle, and his repeated radio calls now made no contact either.

The Chinese might now be entrenching a replacement unit along the slopes the battalion had just cleared. There was no way to see what went on farther north, or know what waited to the south. With no way to contact regimental headquarters, the battalion could not hope for air support to help it to reduce the enemy's defenses and get through the whole length of the valley tomorrow with minimum losses. Without air support, the colonel expected it would cost the battalion more serious losses if it tried to move northward again through the valley.

Now well south of the gap and in a wide part of the valley floor, the battalion stopped and the men dug into a defensive perimeter, in an open area, near the road, but away from the low hills that bordered the valley floor. Foxholes and slit trenches were dug and crew-served and vehicle-borne weapons positioned in the perimeter's center, where they could be aimed quickly in any direction.

Around the perimeter, the 30-cal. machine guns of the battalion's infantry companies were positioned in fox holes. Two men, some with BARs and some with M-1 rifles, manned each foxhole around the perimeter. In addition, because of the low temperature, the time for which each man in the perimeter was expected to be watchful was reduced to two hours at a time.

By then the sky was nearly cloudless and a full moon shone in a star bedecked heaven that would have been a joy to an astronomy amateur, if he could have stopped thinking about the coldness, for the temperature plunged to minus 20 degrees Fahrenheit. The men, clad in summer uniforms, were miserable. Frostbite was too willing a companion, and those that slept soundly for too long, froze to death. Others suffered permanently disabling injuries, such as the loss of toes, feet, and fingers. One-third of the men were on guard, while the others rested, and hopefully did not sleep too soundly.

At about 400 hours, in the early morning, the men on guard and those sleeping lightly and uncomfortably were snapped fully alert by the din of bugles, whistles, rattles, drums, and of shouting soldiers that charged towards their outer perimeter. Chinese soldiers rose from the ground along the bottom of the tree line of the hill to the battalion's west and swarmed towards Company D's positions, shouting, making noise, and firing rifles, burp guns, Thompson sub-machine guns, and katyusha rockets, throwing concussion grenades as they came. At the same time, enemy mortar rounds exploded inside the perimeter.

Even though the men inside the perimeter had been certain the Chinese were in the area, the explosions, shouting, and shooting jolted them and caused momentary confusion amongst them. Within Company D, which faced the full weight of the Chinese charge, it caused panic.

GIs in the perimeter's outer ring began to fire at the Chinese. Because of the sheer numbers in the Chinese ranks, the GIs fire seemed not to have any effect. For the massed attack continued, at a run, towards the perimeter, with bugles and whistles blowing, and the sound of drums, rattles, shouted orders or oaths, and Chinese small arms fire, along with Chinese mortar and rocket fire, as the attackers neared the outermost US defense.

Before the attackers reached the outermost foxholes and trenches, which lay about 150 yards from the innermost defense perimeter and more than 200 yards from the battalion's command post, many GIs of Company D threw down their weapons and fled back through the camp and into the darkness beyond. An officer and a sergeant grabbed at some to try to stop their flight. They managed to calm only a few enough to return them to the fight.

The men of the companies on each side of Company D overcame their panic quickly. From their foxholes and trenches they directed a storm of machine gun, BAR, and rifle fire at the Chinese.

Two-thirds of the crews of the tanks and the half-tracks, with their interlocking 50-cal. machine guns, had been asleep next to their vehicles, while the other crew members were awake in the vehicles. Even with this degree of readiness, it took a minute or more in the darkness for many GIs to understand where the enemy was and to begin to fire at them.

"Quad 50s" in use as infantry-support weapons. The four, vehicle-mounted 50 cal. machine guns were used to support infantry, in Korea.

U.S. Army photo

By the time the battalion's mortar crews began to drop rounds amongst the attackers, and the M-16s, each with two inter-locking 40-mm anti-aircraft cannons, began to fire at point-blank range at the Chinese, the enemy had breached the outer perimeter and was amongst the foxholes and trenches of the inner perimeter.

Many explosions lit the night and shook the ground sometimes sending men tumbling off balance. The air vibrated strongly, causing lungs to compress. Chinese losses were very heavy. Despite this, in what seemed to be seconds, the surviving Chinese swarmed on towards the perimeter's mid-point and battalion headquarters like an unstoppable tidal wave. Many GIs who had slept there only moments before were quickly on their feet, or kneeling on one knee and firing at the oncoming figures that were clad in lighter-colored uniforms than the GIs wore.

The battle raged in complete confusion within the perimeter's center. Explosions lit the night sky, shook the ground, and compressed lungs. Nostrils and mouths were filled with the acrid smell of cordite, and the ears were assaulted by the noise of shouts, screams, and the sound of small arms and machine gun fire.

The ground shook again and again from the impact of rounds fired from the tanks' main guns and from thunderous explosions as those rounds exploded and from the noise of machine guns and rifles' firing. Added to this was the noise of Chinese mortar rounds exploding inside the camp and US mortar rounds exploding from the outer perimeter on outwards toward where the hill's slope met the valley's floor. The air was oppressive and the powerful smells and sound of death and wounds added to its weight. The smell of fear was in the air.

The tank and anti-aircraft gun crews were able to fire at targets within the perimeter for only two to three minutes. After that, the smoke and confused mix of enemy and US troops within the perimeter made it impossible to fire without killing both friend and foe.

The initial panic felt by most men of Company D had become uncontrolled fear and noncoms and officers had followed their men as they fled. Company D was new. Its personnel had been sent to bring the battalion up to its table-of-organization strength, just before the Inchon landing. The ambush yesterday had been its first firefight, and it had done well, after Capt. Wilson took immediate command of it.

Despite the wholesale desertion, the company's commanding officer, a lieutenant, and several sergeants had stood their ground, each an isolated island surrounded by enemy soldiers, and fired at the Chinese, until they were cut down.

MacKenzie noticed a weaponless GI about 15 feet to his right. The man appeared to be overcome by shock and fear and was running from the fighting, screaming a stream of syllables that were not understandable English.

Many of the enemy reached battalion headquarters and continued through the camp to the other side. Some attacked the GIs clustered around tanks and anti-aircraft vehicles. Those GIs that had stood their ground and defended the camp had fought furiously against the attackers, but without any unit organization. In the darkness, the smoke from weapon muzzles had added to the difficulty of organizing a defense and made it almost impossible to identify foe from friend, until figures were within a few yards. Because of this, GIs sometimes shot at figures they thought were enemy and killed or wounded other GIs.

Only in the area around the tanks and anti-aircraft vehicles was it possible to know, at a distance of even 15 feet, which figure was the enemy and which a GI. In that part of the camp, the battle developed into vicious hand-to-hand combat, with GIs using bayonets, rifle butts, and hand-held bayonets to repel attackers.

One of the tanks blew up with a roar and tremendous flash of light. The explosion's vibrations shook the ground, knocked nearby men to the ground, killing and wounding some, and buffeted men farther away with shock waves of air that compressed their chests and forced air from their lungs. The blast was caused by an explosive charge placed by a Chinese soldier, where it first caused the tank's engine to burn and then caused the tank to explode.

What seemed to be only a moment later, flames shot up from two trucks parked on the far side the battalion's command post. Around the camp, at all points, it seemed as if the noise of battle sounded.

Gradually, the noise lessened and, after more than an hour, the surviving Chinese ran back through the camp, their weapons in their hands, to the hill from which they had emerged. About 40 to 50 Chinese moved from the inner perimeter towards the hill more slowly than the rest of the survivors of their unit, which had quickly reached the hill and disappeared among the bushes and trees there. They may have been walking wounded. GIs fired at them, and the anti-aircraft guns and remaining tank's canon added their fire and cut down many. As the main body of surviving Chinese retired from the camp, sporadic fighting within the camp continued for a few minutes, as GIs tracked down and killed the handful of armed Chinese that remained there.

The report of firearms slackened, then stopped, and smoke from the shooting, along with the strong cordite smell, drifted away. As the shooting lessened, it became possible to make out an occasional individual voice from the sounds of men talking. The voices were US officers and sergeants organizing their squads, platoons and companies and directing GIs to re-take possession of the perimeters. The battalion had held.

Among the voices were the sounds of seriously wounded men. Some moaned. Others screamed and writhed in pain.

Strewn in a path from the hill into the camp were the bodies of dead Chinese, as well as some very seriously wounded ones. A battlefield survey showed that more than 280 of the enemy had been killed, and nearly three dozen badly wounded ones lay among their dead comrades. The fight to defend the camp and drive off the Chinese was a tarnished victory for the battalion. It had lost 68 men dead and another 280 wounded.

In addition, Company D no longer existed. Fewer than 20 of its 177 men were accounted for, and most of those were dead on the battlefield. The others were gone and with them, many men from other companies. They had either been taken prisoner or run away in panic. The battalion had also lost a medium tank with its 90-mm main gun and 50-cal. machine gun, two 2-1/2-ton trucks, and a jeep.
Not only was the battalion's combat strength seriously depleted, but ammunition was also a concern. There was enough left for one more battle, but not more. The damage done to the battalion's morale was

probably more serious. The heavily armed battalion had been savaged in two battles in fewer than 24 hours by men clad in cloth shoes, and, when armed, armed with old Japanese and Russian-made rifles, burp guns, US-made Thompson sub-machine guns, and light mortars.

GIs look at Chinese dead killed during a massed attack.

National Archive

The GIs had been surprised earlier in the valley, and, as a result, had prepared the camp's defenses well, but not well enough to prevent massive numbers of Chinese from overrunning it at one point in the perimeter and penetrating beyond battalion headquarters. Col. McClusky gathered the company commanders' reports and estimated the attackers had numbered no more than 500 to 700 men when they first attacked.

The battalion's medics worked steadily with the supplies they had to tend the wounded. They made those they could do nothing for as comfortable as they could with injections of morphine and moved on to help those they could help to survive. The seriously wounded were carried to one of the trucks and placed on its bed.

Because the remaining trucks were needed to carry seriously wounded men, heavy weapons, and ammunition, the colonel ordered a trench dug in a flat area near the road. Dog tags were taken from the corpses for report purposes, and the newly dead were buried, along with the dead from the first battle. The place was carefully recorded, so the bodies could be recovered at a later time.

Capt. Wilson walked through the company's positions to see the condition his men were in and talk with some. He also talked with several of the wounded and ordered more ammunition carried to the machine gun crews, BAR teams, and riflemen.

Some of the men needed clean trousers, for they had pissed or shat in theirs when the attack began suddenly. Unfortunately, none were available, so they did the best they could, and the smell of urine and feces joined the battalion, until frost eliminated it for a while.

When Capt. Wilson reported to Col. McClusky along with the other company commanders, he found the battalion commander, intelligence officer, and operations officer examining a paper that had been left on a table in the battalion's command post. When Capt. Wilson entered, the colonel looked at him grimly and held up the paper. He said, "Look at this! It was left here as a calling card, but none of us can read it. Can your man help?"

Capt. Wilson looked at it and said, "Sir, all I see is pictograms. I can't tell what any of them mean, but I do know this is not Korean writing. These pictograms are either Chinese or Japanese, and since the attackers were Chinese, it's a safe bet this is Chinese writing. Let me get Heidey here to tell us what we have."

The captain sent a GI to get Heidey, who was with Company B, in the same platoon as MacKenzie. The soldier returned with another soldier who had eastern Asian features and complexion, and who bowed to the captain and asked what the captain wanted.

"Heidey, can you tell us if this writing is Japanese or Chinese?"

"Yes, sir," said Heidey, taking the paper. In just a few seconds he looked at the captain and said, "Chinese, sir."

"Are you certain, Heidey?" asked Capt. Wilson.

"Yes, sir. Very certain," said Heidey, in good English that had a noticeable Japanese accent. "The pictograms are like Japanese Kanji pictograms, but one must read them differently."

"Can you read any of them?" asked the captain.

"I can read them, but not with certainty as to what their meaning is in Chinese," said Heidey.

"Thank you, Heidey. That is all."

At that, Heidey, bowed, turned, and returned to Company B.

"It's certain then," said the colonel. "We can send it to regiment with our report and say the attacking unit was definitely Chinese. I hope they have this translated and word of the new enemy is sent quickly and clearly, so the supreme commander understands we have a new enemy.

"What is curious about the attack is that, after overrunning our battalion command post, the attackers left our maps and code books untouched. We have found everything here that we had here before the attack. Nothing appears to be missing."

"What do you make of it, sir?" Capt. Wilson asked.

"There is a message here somewhere, but I am not certain what it is. My best guess is that we are being warned not to advance, but that's just a wild guess."

"If this information reaches Tokyo, I would like to see the faces there. They are still proclaiming confidently that the Chinese will not dare to intervene. According to Tokyo, these Chinese are only volunteers and there are not more than 30,000 of them. Last week division assured us that no major Chinese units were in Korea. They said our air reconnaissance had not spotted any major troop or supply movements crossing the Yalu.

"A staff officer with division told me, before Thanksgiving, that he met an Air Force pilot when he was in Seoul, and the pilot said the Air Force had seen tens of thousands of men moving across the Yalu, from China into North Korea. At that time, they had seen the movement for several weeks and reported it. Gen. MacArthur seems to have decided the Chinese will not enter and does not want to believe any contrary evidence. He prefers to think they are coolies carrying supplies to North Korea."

Elsewhere, on the western side of northern North Korea that morning, Chinese had made similar attacks with even more devastating results. They had jolted awake other US units farther south, in the same region, with bugles, whistles, drums, rattles, and gunfire. They had dashed through poorly defended camp perimeters into US Army camps, and overrun both infantry and gun positions. They had killed and wounded many US soldiers and sent the survivors running in fear and panic, throwing away their helmets, weapons, and other equipment, in order to flee faster. Relatively large numbers of GIs had been taken prisoner, mostly men that had run from their units.

As the next day dawned, 14 of the battalion's men who had been unaccounted for straggled back into the battalion's camp. Each told a different story about how he had become separated from the battalion. Col. told his company commanders to note the names of these men and take no action against them, if they performed satisfactorily during the rest of the campaign. Each one was, however, subjected to some degree of humiliation, for they were assigned to take the place of dead or wounded men in the companies that had stood fast. Each also received a private dressing down by his new platoon commander and platoon sergeant and a warning about what would happen if he did not obey all orders and stand fast no matter what battle condition he found himself in.

None of the other missing men were seen again. Some may have been captured and died before reaching a prison camp. Others may have died of wounds, exposure, or exhaustion in the desolate, frigid hills.

A work detail from Company C, led by a platoon sergeant, was sent to retrieve deserters' weapons and other equipment needed to re-equip the returned men, as well as all small arms ammunition that could be found. The detail consisted of one squad to retrieve equipment and two more to protect them. The path taken by the panic-stricken men was easy to follow, for they left a trail of weapons, helmets, and other equipment that began within the camp and led out away from the camp, as each man lightened his load in headlong flight into the night.

It took the work party only ten minutes to gather enough equipment to fully re-equip the men who had returned with only the uniforms they wore. Each was given a full issue of equipment needed to take part in the next battle: including web belt, bayonet, first aid kit, rifle, ammunition, helmet, canteen, and mess kit. Blankets for them were available in the camp area.

This was the battalion's first experience with desertion under fire, a situation that was so frequent in army units in Korea at this time that men called it "bugging out," instead of desertion. Returning deserters were not treated severely until well into 1951.

Within the perimeter, Smith and MacKenzie looked at the corpse of a dead Chinese soldier.

"Look at this," said Smith, as he held up with his hand part of the quilted, brown jacket of the dead Chinese soldier. "This feels like cotton, and look at his feet. He has on cloth shoes with rubber soles. That's all we've seen on any Chinese corpses. How do they keep their feet from freezing? And look at the other corpses! The same cotton uniforms and shoes! There must be some kind of Asian anti-freeze given these men to keep them from feeling the temperature the way we do."

The dead GIs had been carefully laid out and then buried. Bodies not laid out quickly froze in the sometimes grotesque positions in which the men had died or been killed.

Bodies not laid out quickly froze, in those positions in which the men had died or been killed. Chinese soldiers had taken footwear and clothes from some of the corpses shown here.

U.S. Marine Corps Photo

As the next day dawned, frigid and grey, a brisk north wind whipped over the men. Lt. Lauterbach returned to his tent from a meeting with Capt. Wilson. Smith entered the tent a moment later, and the lieutenant told him the latest news.

"Master Sgt. Beaudreau, the company's first sergeant, was killed yesterday, and Capt. Wilson agrees you should take over the position. I have tapped MacKenzie to take over as platoon sergeant for 2nd Platoon. Good luck. I know you all will carry out your duties well.

"And Smith, get your gear together and report to Capt. Wilson. But before you go, find MacKenzie and tell him to report to me. I want to tell him about the promotions and have him recommend a squad leader to replace him in charge of his squad."

It took Smith only a few minutes to gather his gear. Then he left the tent he and the lieutenant shared and walked over to where MacKenzie was cleaning his rifle with a tooth brush.

"Good morning, Mac," he said. "Congratulations!"

"Good morning. And why congratulations? What is the battalion's situation?"

"Congratulations, because you have been promoted to platoon sergeant of 2nd Platoon. I have been promoted to company first sergeant of Company B, replacing Beaudreau, who was killed yesterday. Get your things together and report to Lt. Lauterbach."

MacKenzie said nothing, just looked at Smith.

"You don't seem interested. You might as well accept the promotion. This war shows no preference for killing company-grade officers, noncoms, or privates, so why not earn a platoon sergeant's pay?

"As for the situation, as far as I know, no one really knows what it is. We have no contact with regimental headquarters. Early this morning, the colonel sent a recon patrol back down the road to try to find it. They drove back to where we thought it might be and found the camp was gone.

"The colonel reorganized the battalion, so there are now three platoons in Company A and two each in companies B and C. Our last order was to move north to Yongby'on, which is just south of the road that runs up to the Yalu. We're supposed to move out shortly. He wants Companies A and B to move ahead of the vehicles and clear out any Chinese positions they find blocking the gap. When they find blockage, they will have full support from every weapon at our disposal. Company C will be in reserve."

MacKenzie said "Thanks" and nodded his head to acknowledge he understood.

Smith said, "Good luck, Mac. I'll see you later." He turned to leave and then turned again towards MacKenzie.

"Hey Mac, I forgot to ask you who you think should fill your position as squad leader. Who do you think is the best qualified?"

Without hesitation, MacKenzie said, "Darden is the right man."

"Good! I agree. I'll give that information to the lieutenant."

Smith turned again and walked away in the direction of the company tent, and MacKenzie gathered his gear. Within a few minutes, he was at the lieutenant's tent to report for his new duties. He announced his presence by saying loudly to the tent flaps used as an entrance and exit: "Sgt. MacKenzie reporting for duty sir."

Lt. Lauterbach told him to enter. The lieutenant was seated on his helmet, with the flat top of an empty ammunition container on his knees, finishing a drawing, on paper, of what looked like a map of the terrain they were in, the gap to the north, and the valley beyond.

"Hi, sergeant. I guess Sgt. Smith told you he was pulled up to serve in the company first sergeant's position, You have done an excellent job as a squad leader, and I reckon you and I will be able to work as smoothly together as Smith and I did. What do you think?"

"I'll be right pleased to serve as platoon sergeant, sir," said MacKenzie.

Shortly after that, the battalion packed its gear and began to move forward. A and B Companies moved ahead with the tank. A short distance from the gap, mortars and howitzers were moved into positions to provide covering fire for the advancing infantry.

Companies A and B moved into the gap and through it. Each company climbed the slopes on one side of the gap to look for Chinese. Each advanced in this fashion, with armor on the valley floor, ready to fire when requested to do so. Neither company found any Chinese.

The battalion's vehicles had moved into the valley behind them and on northward. The battalion's last order from regiment had been to move through the valley and link up with the regiment's other units, at the road junction north of Yongby'en, well north of the Congchon River. Despite the fact that contact with regimental headquarters could not be made, the colonel continued the battalion's northward move towards the assigned meeting point. That day, the battalion moved northward unopposed through the valley in which it had been ambushed the day before.

By late afternoon, they reached the point where a road runs eastward from Pakch'on to the Yalu, and westward to a coastal road that runs to Anju and Sinanju on the southern side of the Chongchon. If the old Japanese map, which was the only map of Korea available, was accurate, they were then probably 30 miles north of the Chongchon.

The battalion halted its forward movement and made camp several hundred feet southeast of the crossroad. They were several miles north of the valley they had come through and at the meeting point. Vehicles and men were again positioned within concentric perimeters and in fox holes that ensured there would be overlapping fire fields. The precautions taken were, however, more stringent than before.

"Capt. Wilson says we're to dig every fox hole a foot deeper than we've been digging them, just in case more Chinese attack," MacKenzie told men of his platoon, as he briefed them about the latest order. "BAR and machine gun crews will be positioned in the inner perimeter, with fox holes of the inner perimeter covering openings between the outer ones."

"What will we do at dawn?" one soldier asked.

"I don't know more than I just told you all. My best guess, right now, is that we will move out to meet regiment tomorrow."

MacKenzie could not help thinking how the perimeters resembled settlers moving through the American west circling a wagon train on prairie for protection, or Afrikaaners laagering their wagons for the same purpose, while trekking towards a new homeland and away from English domination.

He called out a squad from the platoon and told the men they would go on a patrol that night to determine the terrain that lay ahead and identify enemy positions, if they came near any. They were to avoid combat, unless necessary to get back to battalion.

"Heidey!" MacKenzie called, and Heidey stood where he had squatted with the men of another squad. He came to MacKenzie and bowed. "Heidey, I want you to go with this patrol and make one of the excellent maps you make of what you see."

"Yes, sergeant," said Heidey, with another bow.

6

HIDEAKI WATANABI

Heidey was one of a kind, and the battalion reckoned him a treasure. No other battalion had anyone like him, nor did any regiment, nor division. At least, not that anyone knew about. His full name was Hideaki Watanabi, but the Americans, with their inability, or unwillingness, to master non-English words and names, and bent for familiarity, immediately shortened it to Heidey. He was 29-years old when he first saw Capt. Wilson at the battalion's quarters in Yokohama, and offered to do whatever cleaning, painting, or other work the captain or the company wanted done.

Heidey said he had been a medic in the Japanese army during World War II, and had been stationed on Formosa and then in Korea. Capt. Wilson had no need of Heidey's medical or military experience, but the man appeared so mature, presentable, personable, and eager that the captain decided to give him a chance. The company could use someone to do the odd jobs that it otherwise took the base's maintenance department ages to do.

Heidey quickly proved himself to be prompt, careful, and complete in carrying out every request made of him. He was able to do carpentry, electrical wiring, and plumbing repairs, and chores such as washing the captain's car and wrapping packages for the men to mail home to the US. His varied skills and pleasantness quickly made him a valued part of the company's daily life.

Heidey had unexpectedly great skill as an artist and painted a full color painting on a large wall over the chow line, inside the enlisted men's mess. The mess hall painting showed US troops in combat, complete with fighter aircraft swooping out of the sky in close ground support. The painting appeared three dimensional and was popular with the men.

Later, Heidey would paint decorative, cheerful, Japanese-style murals on a wall in each of the company's barracks. Above and beyond these skills and talents, Heidey spoke English well.

A good example of Heidey's dedication to any task asked of him was the mess hall painting. It covered the full width of the wall on the inside of the building over the chow line, where food was served into the men's metal mess trays. The painting was only partly finished when the captain looked at it and complimented Heidey.

"It certainly is a fine looking painting. It looks so three-dimensional I can feel the battle raging. It certainly is realistic looking. It's too bad it won't be finished by the time the division's commanding general visits us next week."

Several days later, the captain came into the mess hall extra early to inspect the kitchen area and found Heidey asleep under the painting, curled up inside an empty potato sack for warmth. He awakened Heidey and asked if he was well, and Heidey told him he was fine. Heidey explained he had worked through the night to finish the painting and had gone to sleep there because it was too late to get public transportation to Tokyo, where he lived with his parents.

Later that day, the captain had the company's first sergeant find room for a cot, foot locker, and metal locker for Heidey. The place found was in the storage room, in one of the company's barracks. It had a door, and only Heidey and the company's first sergeant had the key to its lock. It would do for Heidey's use when late afternoon assignments made it inconvenient for him to travel to Tokyo.

Once the room was available, Heidey became even more of a fixture with the company. He already ate with the men in the mess hall, and now the captain noticed Heidey in the chapel on Sundays, when he went there with his family for the main service. Heidey was not a Christian, but was interested in everything intrinsically American, and he studied Reformation Christianity from the outside, so to speak, because he had decided it was a basic element in America's ethical and moral fiber.

He revered Douglas MacArthur as one of the greater sages in the world's history, and was convinced the changes he had made in Japan were all for the better.

He also attended, as his work assignments allowed, the various fast-pitch softball games the company's team played against other companies, and the games between the base's team and visiting teams from other bases. In addition, he read many US magazines and newspapers. His interest in the US was common knowledge amongst the soldiers, and he was the beneficiary of every magazine and newspaper they had read and no longer wanted.

Heidey's knowledge of the US was far deeper than superficial fascination. He read books about the way the US was governed, at the various levels, and usually knew more about current, US-national-political news than most US servicemen, whose main interests were short persons who wore skirts.

His knowledge became evident only when a US serviceman engaged him in conversation. At those times, he would very diplomatically say what he had read and heard about an event, without disclosing his own judgment about it. Everyone agreed Heidey would make a good ambassador for Japan to another country: particularly the US, or from the US to another country.

Such was Heidey's devotion to the work assigned him, that Capt. Wilson could count on him to complete every request well and on time. He was more conscientious than most men in the company, who, as noted, were more interested in free-time, off-base activities than their assigned military duties.

When the battalion was ordered to pack and move to Korea, Capt. Wilson listened politely to Heidey's heartfelt plea to be allowed to go with the company. The captain told Col. McClusky about the request, and the colonel, who knew about Heidey, said to go ahead, but be certain no one outside the battalion knew.

Just before the battalion left to board LSTs for the three-day-long journey to southeastern Korea, Heidey was issued a complete field uniform and equipment, including rifle and ammunition. When Company B boarded the LST, Heidey appeared to be just another GI in a long line of GIs filing aboard. To ensure success for the venture, Col. McClusky put Capt. Wilson in charge of the men who checked off each person and piece of equipment that went aboard. Capt. Wilson, in turn, chose men he knew well, from Company B, to work under him to do the checking off.

In Korea, Capt. Wilson kept Heidey in the company's rear when moving into a possible firefight. However, when a patrol was sent to reconnoiter, Heidey was usually with it. He would return each time with a map of the area patrolled that was of such fine quality that the battalion knew even the relative elevation and contours of the area drawn, as well as where NKPA positions had been spotted.

It was only after the battalion had landed in Korea that the captain learned Heidey spoke Korean. That happened as a result of a night patrol Heidey went on, which met several hundred Korean refugees that were headed straight towards the battalion's camp. As his American friends stood aside to let the Koreans pass by, Heidey stepped forward, leveled his rifle at several of the Koreans and spoke to them in Korean. The Koreans stopped, and Heidey told the GIs to cover the refugees with their shoulder weapons.

He then walked to the Koreans, one at a time, and had each to open his or her outer clothing. He found a field radio under the outer garment of one woman who had told him she was pregnant, and shoulder and hand weapons and US-issue fragmentation grenades on three men with her. These were clearly guerillas, and the GIs took them into custody at once as war prisoners.

After that, the GIs called for Heidey whenever they came across refugees. He acquired within the whole battalion the aura a wise man probably acquired in ancient Athens or Sumar. In a real sense, Heidey was the battalion's secret weapon.

Using an escort tank as cover and to steady his aim, a GI fires a Browning Automatic Rifle at sources of enemy rifle and mortar fire.

National Archive

7

NORTHWARD AGAIN

The next morning, Capt. Wilson told his platoon officers to have the men board the trucks. "We sent a recon patrol ahead of us before dawn. It reported trouble some time after it left here," he said. "Then we lost contact with them. The colonel suspects they ran into an ambush, but they should at least have had time to break radio silence and report. Otherwise, they should have been back by now. Their order was to reconnoiter to the north and head back.

"The night patrols, which scouted around us in other directions, reported this morning they had spotted no Chinese positions or patrols. If the area ahead is clear, there should be no problems for a while, but we must be ready for anything.

"The colonel made contact with regiment early today and was told to continue northward.

"There's another matter I want you to note and relay to your platoons. The colonel told me to impress it on you and for you to impress it on the men. It's very important. When we board vehicles again, board the men by the squad and platoon, and keep your platoons in trucks that follow immediately after each other. Platoon commanders are responsible for seeing that their platoons and squads do not become mixed up with others. Is that clear?

"When we were ambushed in the gap, the men in the trucks jumped off and became confused with platoons they were not part of. The colonel was furious, because several officers panicked, at first, and then had to get their men together before an effective defense could be made. He said that cost us a few dead and wounded, and he will not tolerate that happening again."

The battalion had moved northward and nearly to the rendezvous point when it drove up to the wreckage of two jeeps. They had been riddled by machine gun and small arms fire. In and beside the ruined vehicles were the dead bodies of the recon patrol the battalion had lost contact with. It looked as if the men in one jeep had been caught by surprise and killed before they could react to the ambush. The men in the other had apparently begun to return fire, but been cut down quickly.

The GIs' stared grimly at the sight and had little to say. Officers inspected the area and then ordered a squad to take dog tags from the corpses. The jeeps were shoved off the road and the bodies buried in a shallow trench dug by the roadside. The location was then carefully recorded, and the battalion moved northward again.

That evening, after the battalion camped and secured its perimeter, MacKenzie walked over to the fire Smith was near and filled his canteen with hot water. Then he squatted beside Smith and asked, "What's going on Sarge? Is the war almost over, or have the Chinese come in to start it over again?"

Smith hesitated for a moment and then said, "Let me tell you what I reckon I know, right from the beginning of this mess we are in. You've heard much of it before, but I reckon it now seems to be good information and not just rumor.

"At the beginning of November, the Chinese attacked and ripped apart the South Korean II Corps and US units. They chewed up large parts of every unit they attacked. Some units were just badly mauled, but most fell apart and fled in haste and disarray. That panicked other units, and they also fled. You remember how the attacks caught everyone by surprise, because we thought the war was over and all we had to do was reach the Yalu, so we could go home? It was not over, and the result has been catastrophic for us.

"The First Cavalry Division was ordered to engage the enemy and passed northward through the ROK units to do so. What happened then was that the Chinese attacked and ripped them apart. That happened between November 1st and 3rd. Some First Cav units were mauled so badly they are ineffective now as combat units, or at least that is the story I heard from one of our men just back from hospital. He said he talked with some of them before he was started back to us.

"It seems as if the Chinese attacked, for about 10 days, in different places across the whole peninsula. All the attacks I heard about had a similar pattern. Large Chinese units surprised our units and came at them blowing their bugles and whistles, and covered by mortar fire, while firing at us with small arms and rockets and throwing grenades when they came close enough.

"We experienced the same type of attack yesterday. On the day before, we learned the Chinese will ambush, in daylight. But from what I have heard they are too clever to attack head on during the day, unless they think the objective is worth the losses they will sustain. They use night as cover to infiltrate between our units and then attack isolated units on an exposed flank, or attack from behind.

"At far as I know, they won every battle they fought. They had everything going for them. They had driven back or destroyed the whole UN line, and then, as suddenly and unexpectedly as they had attacked, they withdrew. And they seemed to disappear, for our intelligence could not find any significant number of them. Until they hit us."

"How could that happen?" asked MacKenzie. "We have far superior fire power and should have flattened them."

"Yup! You are so right. However, our units panicked and ran. I heard the units that fell apart left their crew-served weapons, ammunition, other equipment, and supplies, in perfect condition. The men and officers took off southward, on foot. They even left their wounded, and many men that fled threw away their rifles and other equipment. We saw panic and desertion happen yesterday in our battalion, on a smaller scale."

MacKenzie said, "When we were first shipped to Korea, we paid dearly for the easy duty we had in Japan. But since then, I reckon, we have become battle hardened and competent soldiers. I can attribute our earlier defeats to the softness and lack of training our units had and to outdated weapons. But I reckon it is now right to say there must be something seriously wrong with the leadership up to the highest levels."

Smith nodded assent. After a pause, he said, "When we were first shoved into this war, our equipment and ordnance were poor compared with what the North Koreans had. But underneath that, it seems to me the basic problem has been poor leadership, poor training, poor scouting, poor field positions, and more poor leadership. You and I know our battalion did not have even one day of battalion-strength field training, while in Japan. Most officers have had to learn everything in combat here, and that has cost us many dead and wounded. But aside from that, I agree that the highest command levels appear to have learned nothing.

"Our battalion's loses have been terrible, but if Col. McClusky was not our battalion commander, I reckon there would be no more battalion, by now. We would have been smashed as easily as other units have been. I reckon the way he has positioned us and posted guards and scouted has helped. His ability to remember his World War II combat experience has made a big difference. We have held and fought back and not panicked and been destroyed the way some units have.

"Of course that leaves a lot of explaining to do about the other officers that were also in combat, during the last war. They are senior officers now. What happened to their experiences? Did they forget everything they learned? Maybe easy duty sapped their memories."

MacKenzie looked concerned as he said, "If the Chinese soldiers in Korea are the men I reckon they are, we are in for some rough times. Especially if MacArthur keeps us headed northward towards the Chinese border. Those Chinese fought a civil war against Chinese war lords and Chang Kai Shek's Nationalists, before World War II. Then they fought the Japanese during that war; and, after that they fought American-equipped Nationalist armies again, until they drove them out of China and onto Formosa. And that was only a bit more than a year ago.

"Red China can muster some of the toughest combat veterans in the world. And it can muster them by the millions. I read somewhere that the Red Chinese enlist as soldiers for life, and that some have been fighting the enemies of Communist ideology for 30 years and more. If men like that are told to stop our advance to China's border, I am certain they will fight like wildcats to destroy us, since they consider us to be the army of a capitalist and imperialist country."

The conversation lapsed again. Then Smith said, "The North Korean army is supposed to be a shattered remnant. I read we have taken about 135,000 of them prisoner, and their total loses have been about 335,000 men. If we really do have 135,000 of them in our prison camps and really killed 200,000 others, that means we have captured and killed the number of soldiers they supposedly had, when they began this war.

"In that case, there is no way North Korea can launch even a division-sized attack against us to stop us from reaching the Yalu. Of course, if we have been told the truth, there should be no more of them left to fight us. But that arithmetic is probably irrelevant now, since the Chinese are in the war."

MacKenzie nodded agreement, and said, "I heard Tokyo estimates there may be 100,000 Chinese north of us, and I heard other estimates that say as many as a million. I surely don't know how many there are just north of us, but I understand China has at least five million men in its army. So, if they have decided to try to stop us here, or to drive us back, they have large numbers of men to try to do it with and can accept huge loses.

"You know, I wonder about how 100,000 Chinese troops and weapons and supplies could move across the Yalu without being detected? We heard rumors about them. The high command in Tokyo must have had information from many sources to document their movements. On top of that, I understand Tokyo has reports about statements made by many Chinese prisoners that there is a very large Chinese military presence south of the Yalu."

"Why did they become involved in the war now?" said Smith.

MacKenzie thought for a moment and then said, "Is it possible the Chinese attacked and battered South Korean and US troops, early in November, to send MacArthur, or Pres. Truman, a message that they do not want our military to occupy the southern side of their border with Korea? Maybe they broke off combat to see if the message registered.

"I heard that when they overran command posts they did not take code books, maps, or anything else used to plan movements. Just the same as they did to us yesterday. If they are in this to throw us out of Korea, they would have grabbed that type of material. There is a rumor that they took prisoners when they attacked other units, and later released them, and let them find their way back to our lines. If that really happened, there would have to be a message in it.

"I reckon they attacked, won, disengaged, and let captured men return to us for to see if MacArthur and Washington could understand their message and stop advancing towards the Yalu. If that is what they wanted to tell us, then their message has not been understood, or is being disregarded, or else we would not have been ordered to move northward again. I am dead sure the Chinese army is ready to attack us again, when we move ahead."

"Interesting analysis," said Smith. "It's as good as any I have heard. The US has no diplomatic relations with Communist China, so the Reds might have had to deliver their message on the battle field. However, right now our high command is certain the war is almost over, or so they keep telling everyone that will listen.

"Meanwhile, a Chinese army is between us and the Yalu, the weather has become frigid, and we have no winter clothing. How does the army expect us to survive, much less be alert, move to the Yalu, and fight, if necessary?"

"I hope we get full winter gear soon," said MacKenzie, closing his summer field jacket at the neck. "If we are exposed to a deep Siberian winter roaring over Korea, it will be so damned cold that the wind will freeze exposed skin, before you know it's frozen. According to the *Guide Book to Korea* I bought in Japan, we're only weeks away from that."

"What do you think, Heidey," Smith said, turning to the Japanese, who was seated with them, listening carefully but silently to the conversation.

"I do not think China would send a small army to fight Americans. I cannot know what number they have sent, but 100,000 would seem to be very few, for an army as large as China's and as primitive as it is. They overwhelmed the Nationalists with discipline, devotion to Communism, and numbers. They feel great dedication to China, which now has no warlords or great corruption. The men China sends against us are dedicated and very willing to die for their beliefs. I think we must expect very hard fighting."

After weighing Heidey's thoughts, Smith went to Capt. Wilson and repeated Heidey's evaluation of the situation. Capt. Wilson decided the evaluation important enough to repeat to Col. McClusky, who found a way to fit it into his daily report to regiment, without revealing the source of the wisdom: a source that officially did not exist. He valued Heidey's thoughts, but felt certain regiment would not appreciate learning that the source was the battalion's smuggled wise man. The colonel had enough problems fighting an enemy armed with deadly weapons, and did not want to fight one armed with paper, forms, typewriters, and regulations.

8

STORM ACOMING

The battalion was up before dawn and quickly made ready to meet other elements of the regiment. It had waited for them for several hours, when, at 1040 hours, a messenger from Capt. Wilson found Lt. Lauterbach and gave him a copy of an order battalion had just received from regimental headquarters, by radio. Lt. Lauterbach read it and then called Smith, MacKenzie, and his other platoon leaders to him and said, "We have been ordered to stop our forward movement and wait here for further orders."

"Any reason given, sir?" asked one of the noncoms.

"None," said the lieutenant, "and Capt. Wilson is with the battalion commander to try to find out what is going on. He should be back soon with some explanation, if battalion can find out."

Early that afternoon, Lt. Lauterbach again called his platoon noncoms together and told them, "The captain came back from battalion headquarters with information that major Red Chinese units are in Korea, and that there are unsubstantiated rumors that they began major attacks on UN forces, across the whole peninsula, before dawn today. The effect of those attacks seems to have been devastating. No one knows how many Chinese are involved, but it appears several more of our units have been surprised, or driven back, and contact has been lost with most South Korean units.

"The Chinese infiltrated between many UN units and got behind them and blocked their retreat. Regiment has not been able to contact division headquarters, since early today, and we are not certain whether or not the units that were on our flanks are there now. At this time, we do not know if we have friendly units on our flanks, or if our flanks are empty, or if there are Chinese there."

That evening, Lt. Lauterbach and MacKenzie called together those platoon members that were not on guard duty. The lieutenant told them, "Col. McClusky and regimental headquarters assume the main body of the Chinese army lies to the north, to block our movement to the Yalu. We know there are also major Chinese units south of us, because, before dawn today, they attacked and surprised units of our division there. They appear to have overrun camp perimeters with great ease and to have inflicted heavy casualties on our personnel.

"In addition, our forces have been driven back with heavy equipment and supply losses. Some units of the division have now retreated to positions several miles south of where they were this morning, and the whereabouts of some units is unknown at this time.

"Most units in the line appear to have fared as badly as or worse than our battalion. There is a report that several South Korean divisions fell apart when attacked. Their movement to the rear was not described as a retreat, but as a disorganized run to get away from the Chinese, just the same as Company D's. They reportedly abandoned everything but their boots as they ran. Several large US units reportedly did the same.

"I reckon we can expect an attack at any time, so we had better be ready. During daylight, the attacks could come in the form of ambushes, or roadblocks, which are reportedly being used. Each night, we must camp within a carefully defended perimeter. If it comes to the point that we must retreat, our retreat must be orderly, and we can expect to be attacked as we retreat.

"If we stay together, in our unit organizations, we will be able to defend ourselves better, and there is a better chance some of us will make it through this alive. If we do not, I'd bet none of us make it back. I have seen you all in combat and am sure I can count on you all to do the right thing at all times. Now, those of you all that don't have guard duty should get some sleep. We want you all to be alert on guard duty and ready to move out tomorrow."

When Smith came by to inspect 2nd Platoon's sector of the perimeter that evening, MacKenzie asked him, "Heard any more news?"

"Just that the South Korean II Corps did fall apart. It was holding about 80 miles of the front. Now there are only Chinese in that gap.

"I did hear a strange story though. The Chinese supposedly overran our lines to the east and killed almost everyone in a regiment there. They took some prisoners that they could just as easily have killed. The Chinese moved on, and when regimental and battalion staffs were able to come back to their command posts, they found nothing missing: not even code books, maps, or orders. And what makes the story even stranger is that the Chinese released their prisoners and let them return to our lines. This is apparently a repeat of what they did earlier."

"I wonder what they had in mind," MacKenzie said.

"Another message MacArthur and his court will be unable to decipher, I suppose," said Smith.

"They act as if they don't really want war with us, but do not want us nearer to their border. I reckon they want to let us know they can stop us and hope our leaders will stop our advance.

"Maybe it is meant for the president and his court?"

The night passed without incident, and early the next morning, when Smith walked through the 2nd Platoon's positions, he told MacKenzie, "Have your men ready to move immediately after breakfast. We have been ordered to move southward to help to close the front and to prevent further Chinese infiltration."

The men nearby stirred and wakened at the sound of Smith's voice. They slept lightly and were attuned to their officers and noncoms voices, even when they appeared to sleep soundly.

"What do you hear, Sarge?" asked MacKenzie.

"The 2nd Division moved southward and reportedly ran into strong road blocks. Infantry have been sent to clear the enemy from hills overlooking the road the division took, but have had no success, so far.

"A regiment northeast of us was attacked at about 400 hours today. I heard the Chinese went through their camp like a hot knife through butter. Thousands of them came a-screaming, while bugles and whistles blew, rattles made noise, drums beat, and commands were shouted to them from every point they were at. After the first surprise, our men cut the Chinese down like a scythe cuts hay, but the Chinese behind the fallen ones kept acoming, until they overran the camp."

"Good googelly mook!" exclaimed DeAngelo, a soldier from Metarie, Louisiana, who was on his feet, across from MacKenzie. DeAngelo's mouth was open slightly, but he said nothing more to emphasize the awe he felt about Smith's information.

"It's spooky today," said McCollum, the man next to MacKenzie. "Them Chinks are behind us, in front of us, and probably on the other side of every hill we pass by. They know where we are and can hit us when they want to. It gives me a creepy feeling. They are just like the North Koreans, except there are more of them."

"What do you mean, they are just like the North Koreans?" asked MacKenzie.

"I mean the North Koreans had armor, artillery, and some aircraft. The Chinks are only lightly armed infantry, but there are huge numbers of them."

"Yup," said MacKenzie. "Totally indoctrinated, seasoned troops, willing to die for Communism."

"Yep, it's spooky and frightening," said McCollum.

"What you said is a good reason to be alert and ready to fire," said MacKenzie. "When they spring a surprise attack on us, we will have very few seconds in which to return their fire and cut them down. It we miss that brief opportunity, they will cut us down."

"Right," said McCollum, and shoved the safety on his rifle to the off position.

The battalion re-entered the narrow valley to its south and again moved by the burned, bullet riddled jeeps of the recon patrol. Farther south in the valley, where it narrowed more, the battalion came upon wreckage created after they had headed northward through the same area yesterday. There were burned trucks, abandoned howitzers, destroyed tanks and jeeps, and dead GIs in vehicles and along the roadside. It looked as if a unit of regimental size, or larger, had been destroyed.

The carnage was strewn along the road for more than five miles. The battalion stopped several times to destroy howitzer breeches and tank canon and to search for survivors. The colonel ordered details to scavenge for ammunition and food. Nearer the gap, near the valley's southern end, the battalion passed the wreckage of its own vehicles.

That evening, the battalion encamped near its earlier camp and secured its perimeter. The temperature was below zero and a wind whipped in from the north to make it much colder. The men were yet in summer field uniforms and there had been no re-supply of food or ammunition for a week. Despite what they had scavenged, rations were short. As a result, the men were ordered to eat half their normal daily C rations, until they were re-supplied.

As they ate, Col. McClusky walked amongst his men and talked with many of them. The walk-through gave him a chance to size up the soldiers' morale and see their physical condition.

His message to them was, "You all have given a good account of yourselves in every battle we have fought. You all are brave men and led by brave and capable officers and non-commissioned officers. We are also well armed and battle-seasoned, and our enemy is poorly armed and equipped.

"Our battalion fought well around the Pusan Perimeter, at a time when many men on our side though we could not beat the non-stop, suicidal, frontal attacks by North Korean tank and infantry units. As a result, we were chosen to land at Inchon to relieve the pressure on the Perimeter and to rout the North Koreans.

"We have proven ourselves to be disciplined and highly competent soldiers. Keep up the good work, and we'll give the people back home more good reasons to be proud of us."

"To hell with the people back home," said one soldier quietly to the man next to him. "They don't care about this war or us, and I don't care about this war or Korea, or what the people back home think."

"Holy shit," said one soldier near MacKenzie, "the colonel really put what has happened to us in a different perspective than I experienced."

"Yup. Bless his soul," said MacKenzie. "Consider it to be a pep talk, like the ones given at Friday evening pep rallies, before Saturday football games. And everything he said it true. He just left out the negative side of it.

9

SOUTHWARD AGAIN

The next morning, the battalion rolled towards where the valley narrowed and formed another gap, which the road ran through and then turned at an angle. The hills here were relatively low, varying from under 800 feet to more than 1,100.

There were so many seriously wounded on the trucks that some combat fit riflemen had to ride on the tank or cram onto the remaining half-track.

Burned vehicles and discarded weapons and ammunition along the road witnessed that a US unit had been in a firefight, or been ambushed here, and routed. Amongst the vehicles and along the road GIs corpses lay where they had fallen.

Col. McClusky ordered the corpses put onto trucks, atop the loads of ammunition and equipment in them. He also stopped the battalion several times to have the GIs pick up BARs, ammunition, and grenades that could be found on vehicles, corpses, and along the road, where they had been thrown by men intent on lightening their burdens as they fled in panic. A disabled M-19 gave up a treasure trove of ammunition for 50-cal. machine guns. Elsewhere mortar rounds for light mortars were found.

At one stop, the growing load of corpses was unloaded, dog tags were removed from them, and the corpses were buried in a hastily dug trench a short way from the road. There was no ceremony, but the location was carefully recorded.

During one of these stops, MacKenzie inspected the rifles and ammunition of the men in his squad. He was disappointed, but not surprised, to find two men had not fired any rounds. They had moved in action with the squad, but, for whatever reason, had not fired at the enemy. MacKenzie took each one separately away from his men and, as privately as he could, explained the need for each man to aim at the enemy and shoot, as the army had taught him to do. He explained the importance to the battalion of having every weapon in use to kill enemy soldiers, before they killed him or his comrades. Then he sent each back to the squad, but wondered if his talk would change their behavior.

Farther along the road, a disabled tank supplied main tank-gun ammunition. The tank had been driven off the road, into a shallow roadside ditch. It seemed to be in working condition and well fueled. Col. McClusky ordered it thoroughly destroyed, and a thermite grenade was exploded in its main gun to destroy its usefulness. GIs also used large stones to thoroughly damage the machine gun mounted on its turret. Burning it would have been easier, but the colonel wanted no fires lit at this time, not even to destroy equipment the Chinese might find useful.

Later that day, the battalion came under fire again, this time from the eastern slope of a hill that neared the road. The weary infantry off-loaded and began to return fire. MacKenzie knelt, in turn, by each of the two squad members that had not fired in action and talked each through aiming and firing at the enemy. The mortar crews set up their weapons, fired, and zeroed them in on suspected enemy positions. The tank's main guns, the half track's quad 50-cal guns, and the twin 40-mm cannon zig-zagged their fire across the slopes.

The noise level rose and ground and air vibrated. Eardrums were hurt as the air's rapid and violent vibrations assaulted eardrums and momentarily made inaudible all other sounds. In just minutes, the sounds of weapons firing could no longer be separated from rounds exploding. Arm signals were the only certain way to give commands to men more than two to three yards away, for shouted commands could not be heard. Only mouth movements could be noticed.

Col. McClusky had positioned the infantry in the valley, with the battalion's vehicles, and facing the Chinese held hillside. Companies B and C were ordered to climb the hill and kill all Chinese there that did not surrender. The officers and men of companies B and C formed a skirmish line on the road, and with bayonets fixed, advanced across a frozen creek and onto the hill's lower slope. From the road, Company A, the tracked vehicles, and mortars pounded the hill.

On the hillside, the infantrymen clattered up the stony slope, thinly covered with small trees and bushes. A few hundred feet from the base, the hill's vegetation thinned. At that point, the GIs became the targets of Chinese small arms and machine gun fire from above.

The truck laden with some seriously wounded men was struck by a Chinese rocket or mortar round, and its gas tank exploded in flames. Wounded men screamed in terror, and those that could jumped from the truck's bed. Medics jumped onto the bed and shoved seriously wounded men off onto the snowy road. There was no way to fight the fire, and it cremated the few men the medics could not rescue. Only the medics' heroism prevented more deaths from the fire.

For nearly 45 minutes the infantry worked its way up the slope. Falling snow and blowing, drifting snow made their progress difficult. Lt. Lauterbach led the 2nd Platoon, flanked to the north by Company B's other platoon and to the south by Company A. During that time, the battalion's men and weapons in the valley concentrated heavy fire on the hill above their advancing comrades.

Where the GIs found living Chinese, they shot, bayoneted, and grenaded their way past them to about 450 feet above the valley floor. As the 2nd Platoon moved up hill, a mortar round exploded just ahead of men on MacKenzie's right. It blew stone, branches and earth in every direction and, for a moment, darkened the sky on that side. The debris and vibrations caused several men to lose their footing and slide or fall several feet down hill. Their faces, hands, and summer field uniforms were hit by a hail of debris that moved through the air with the speed of projectiles. The debris ripped and punctured their uniforms and them in numerous places. The men that had lost their footing slowly got to their knees, and faced up hill again. But they were dazed and bleeding.

At that point, fire from a Chinese machine gun, farther up the slope, made progress deadly, for it was positioned on a part of the hill that jutted out and enabled the gun crew to rake the slope wherever targets presented themselves.

MacKenzie's squad was the nearest US unit to the machine gun. The men were crouched on the slope or lying flat against it when Sgt. Smith, who was with them, turned towards MacKenzie and said, in a hoarse whisper, "Hay, Mac, you like hunting?"

"What you got in mind, Sarge?"

"That machine gun is above us and down the valley some distance. If we can take it out, we will have a controlling position and be able to fire into Chinese positions below and on the other side of it. That gun appears to be dug into an emplacement in the hill and protected against anything but a direct hit with a round, or lucky hits with stone and steel fragments. We must destroy it or we'll be stuck here and be hamburger before tomorrow dawns. You and one of your men come with me and give me covering fire."

"Sure 'nuf, Sarge."

MacKenzie turned to Darden, who was next to him, flattened himself against the hill, and told Darden what they were going to do with Sgt. Smith. Then he said, in jest, "Now don't you go and get shot, yuh hear. You're into me fur $500 right now."

"Don't sweat it, Sarge. I always pay my debts. Besides, as best I can tell, the Chinese are lousy shots with rifles."

"I know, but take special care today. I want you to make it to at least three or four more paydays."

"Hell! So do I."

Then Smith said, "Let's go!" and the three moved upwards and somewhat sideways, trying to reach a point almost below the machine gun emplacement. They moved no more than a few feet at a time, feeling for footholds in the stone and dirt and holding on to the trunks of stunted trees, some of which had been shredded by fire from the valley. As they moved, they watched the hill above, ahead, and below for Chinese. Gradually they reached a point almost below the emplacement. Sgt. Smith lay his rifle against a splintered tree trunk and, keeping as low as he could, climbed towards the emplacement. When he reached a point about ten feet below it, rifle fire splattered the hillside near him. He had been spotted.

MacKenzie and Darden searched the hill above and to both sides of them. Through the snowy veil that blew across friend and foe they spotted the enemy rifleman that had fired at Smith. Darden quickly engaged the Chinese soldier in a shooting match. As MacKenzie slammed an ammunition clip into his rifle, the Chinese soldier moved from behind dirt-covered stones he had piled in front of him to aim at Smith, and Darden nailed him with a round through the head.

Smith was now almost directly below the machine gun's position and MacKenzie and Darden waited, at the ready, and searched the slope for enemy. Smith drew from his holster an officer's 45-cal. pistol he had found on one of the battalion's scavenging stops and then pulled the pin on a grenade. That done, he rose with the wild yell of a Southern hunter, so his head and raised arm were above the level of the emplacement, pointed the pistol at the machine gunner, and fired directly into his face and gently lobbed the fragmentation grenade into the emplacement. He fired once more at another Chinese in the emplacement and then slid swiftly downwards towards his rifle.

He had not slid more than five feet below the emplacement when the grenade exploded, and caused ammunition and grenades in the emplacement to explode in a bright flash that shook the air around where the emplacement had been. The blast compressed the lungs of Smith, MacKenzie, and Darden and knocked them off balance. It also blew stones and dirt out of the emplacement and on to snow that lay on the hill around it and onto everything below and on each side of it. Each of them was cut and bruised by debris.

A moment later, Smith, in an overly loud voice, shouted to MacKenzie and Darden, "Follow me!" Both men looked at Smith dazedly, for the blast had temporarily deadened the hearing of each of the three. "Follow me!" Smith repeated and motioned them forward with a wave of his extended right arm. He did not wait, but clattered up onto the carnage of what had been the emplacement and turned and shouted, "Come on you pokes. Move your butts. The view from here is great."

MacKenzie waved to his squad to follow and then moved towards Smith. In moments, he and Darden were on the narrow ledge and the squad was hunkered down just below. As MacKenzie and Darden climbed onto the ledge, Smith was already in a prone position, finding and shooting at targets with deadly effect. Darden did the same, while MacKenzie spread out the rest of his squad and had them find and shoot at targets. In with his squad were two men from another squad who had become detached from their command during the uphill battle's confusion. MacKenzie positioned them also and ordered them to find and shoot at targets.

Smith had shoved the partly disemboweled corpse of a Chinese soldier to the edge of the narrow ledge, from which the blast had blown the emplacement's low, protective wall out onto the hillside. He had rested his rifle on it, and fired at Chinese farther ahead of them. When he paused for a moment and looked at the number of men near him, he shouted to MacKenzie, "For God's sake, spread them out more Mac, or one grenade will get you all. Lead some up higher, and leave Darden with me. Once you all are in position up there"—and he pointed to a raised part of the hill about 90 feet above them—"let me hear a Southron yell, and we'll move ahead."

When Capt. Wilson, at the head of 1st Platoon, reached the hill's crest, the order came from battalion to turn and form a skirmish line from the hill's crest and move southward. Once in position, the infantry moved towards the enemy's positions, on the rest of the long hill.

They had formed and begun to move when the sound of aircraft engines resounded in the valley, and three single-engine Mustang fighter aircraft, with Australian markings, flew in, over a ridge and down from the north. Not one of the aircraft was even 100 feet above the hill's crest. As they flew overhead, the planes' propeller wash sent strong air currents downwards. The currents blew snow into the air and shook leaves, branches, and vegetation that remained on the slope, as well as blowing into the air dirt and vegetation that had been loosened by exploding mortar and tank cannon rounds.

Mustang fighter aircraft of 77 Squadron of the Royal Australian Air Force (RAAF), in flight over Korea . This squadron flew Mustangs early in the Korean War. Later in the war, they flew Meteor jet fighter aircraft.
Photo from RAAF Museum , Cook Point , Victoria , Australia

The pilots strafed and dropped napalm that covered much of the hill ahead of companies B and C. Black clouds of fire trimmed with, and enfolding, orange flames billowed upwards with a roar. Infantry nearest to the napalm cringed and felt searing heat strike them through the freezing air. Then the Mustangs banked to the east and, wing tip to wing tip flew an upside down loop, as if at an air show, banked, circled back, and flew in, in tandem, even lower over the hill as they strafed Chinese positions farther south. After that, they climbed swiftly in a smart "V" formation, dipped their wings in unison to each side, in a salute, and flew away to the south as suddenly as they had appeared.

The air attack happened so quickly and unexpectedly that the GIs had no time to fear the pilots might mistake them for the enemy, which was something every infantryman, early in the war, knew sometimes happened. When the GIs saw what the Australians' first attack had done to any enemy ahead of them, many stood up facing the Mustangs and cheered and waved their helmets to the pilots as they came in to attack again.

Col. McClusky half smiled and half frowned as he watched the Mustangs fly away. He knew the Australians' quick decision to attack had certainly saved a number of his men from death and wounds. He also knew it would have been disastrous if the Australian pilots had not identified the combatants rightly and also understood the direction in which the GIs were attacking.

The battalion had no contact with either regiment or division and no way to request air support, so none had been expected. There was no forward air observer with the battalion to direct the air attacks and no marker out to guide friendly pilots to targets. The Australians' presence was wild luck pure and simple, and it was the Aussies' initiative, skill, and daring that made it so effective.

Not only had the pilots noticed the fighting from afar and correctly identified which side was which and the fighting's direction, but they also had napalm and ammunition aboard which had not yet been used. Maybe they had been sent to support another unit and been unable to find it. Maybe they had been hunting for targets. No one in the battalion knew the answers, but each was thankful the Aussies came when they did. They had prevented casualties in a battalion already low in manpower and ammunition.

MacKenzie was elated too. The Aussies' accuracy had been breathtaking. They had attacked entrenched and well-hidden Chinese and destroyed them from about 100 yards ahead of the GIs to far along the hill. He looked at the burning and smoldering areas ahead of him and reckoned the Aussies had given evidence of unusually excellent eyesight, lightning-fast target analysis, excellent marksmanship, and great flying skill.

A shiver ran through him as he thought about an air attack during a battle on the retreat towards Pusan, when pilots of US jet-fighter planes had swooped in at higher altitudes and much swifter speeds, and napalmed and strafed GIs. He had heard other stories too about other US and allied commands which US fighter aircraft had mistakenly attacked, killing and wounding many US and UN soldiers. It had sometimes seemed that US Air Force ground support was as useful to the enemy as to our side.

The infantrymen climbed down into the valley again and moved farther east, around the smoldering area the Aussies had attacked. As they began to advance up the hillside there, Chinese soldiers entrenched above them fired, and, from the valley, supporting fire from the battalion's units pounded the hill's crest and the area just below it.

Rifle fire crackled on the hillside and an occasional burst of 40-mm rounds or 76-mm tank-cannon rounds churned up dirt, stone, and wood on the slope. There was also the occasional blast of an exploding grenade thrown by one side or the other. Even after the destruction the

GIs advance ready for action, over a hill top scorched by napalm and littered with empty, small-arms-ammunition casings.

U.S. Army photo

Mustangs had wrought on the Chinese, it took Companies B and C more than two more hours to clear the remaining Chinese from the long hill.

When resistance had stopped, the GIs climbed down and rejoined the rest of the battalion. They carried with them their dead and seriously wounded comrades. Medics treated the wounded as best they could with scavenged medical supplies, and then loaded them onto trucks.

Several trucks and jeeps and the tank were all that was left of the vehicles the battalion had moved northward with, for Chinese fire had destroyed the M-19 half track, a truck, and a jeep.

The battalion counted nearly 200 Chinese dead and took prisoner a badly wounded Chinese soldier who died within a few hours.

Amongst the battalion's many dead and wounded in the battle was Heidey, who had been left on the hill's lowest part, just inside where bushes and trees grew. He was too valuable on patrols and for dealing with Koreans to risk in overt attack, and was not in the army. So, his combat activities were limited to the valuable contributions he made on scouting patrols.

Heidey had been hit by a long mortar round intended for the advancing GIs, and his body was in fragments and not easily recognizable as a human corpse. Capt. Wilson had a detail gather every piece of the corpse they could find and bury it by the road, with the dead GIs.

The names of the GIs killed in the fighting were recorded, as was the location of the hastily dug mass grave in which they were buried. This information was part of what was recorded in the company's report, but on the back of a letter from his wife the captain wrote the location and the name "Heidey" next to it. This was the kind of information that would cause division and higher levels to become catatonic, and had to be left encrypted.

Some staff officers at division level, and more the farther from the battlefields one moved, "went by the book"—that is, by the army's huge array of written rules. In combat, however, the first thing officers and men learned was to discard the book. Every rule was adjusted and readjusted to fit new and unexpected situations. There were no fast rules except "take the objective with the fewest possible casualties."

The battle cost the battalion dearly. Col. McClusky had been killed by small arms fire in the fighting's final moments, while giving commands. In the short time the battalion had been north of the Chongchon River, it had lost about 65 percent of its strength, including two captains commanding companies, two lieutenant's commanding platoons and several senior noncoms killed. In addition, several lieutenants and noncoms had been seriously wounded, along with many privates. This resulted in master sergeants being put in command of platoons without officers, as well as in other field promotions at lower command levels.

Capt. Wilson was now the battalion's senior, combat-fit officer and in command of the battalion. He considered the battalion's losses in this last battle acceptable for the results achieved, when compared with the much greater losses it suffered in firefights, since the Chinese attacks began.

However, the captain considered Heidey's death a serious and irreparable blow to the battalion. The competent, unassuming, and willing man who had first joined the company as a handy man and day-worker had been an important part of the fragile flow of information upon which many of the battalion's movements had been decided and the dispositions for battles made. His death would deny the battalion excellent, life-saving intelligence.

For Capt. Wilson and the men of Company B, Heidey's death was also a personal loss. Heidey's cheerful disposition, willingness to do any work requested, and sang froid under combat conditions had often made him a morale booster, for GIs who did not want to be in Korea at all. He had been a trusted friend and boon companion on patrols and in camp and their only communication with the natives. The men also understood his death would seriously limit the information they could now gather on patrols. As a result, Heidey's death was more noticed than that of some GIs, and it cast a grey pall over that day and many more, for every patrol remembered his valuable contributions to their previous successes.

(In 1951, Capt. Wilson had a short leave to visit his wife and children in Japan. While there, he went in full dress uniform to visit Heidey's parents in Tokyo, to tell them how their son died and about the valuable intelligence he had repeatedly gathered for the battalion on patrols in no-man's land, in dealing with refugees, and in reading Korean military documents. He presented them with a combat infantryman's badge, a Korean War medal with four battle stars, the regimental and divisional shoulder badges, and an army fatigue cap. These he bought at the army's post-exchange shop in Yokohama, so Heidey's parents could have some mementos of their son.

(The men of Company B knew about the planned visit, and several gave the captain snapshots, that is, photo prints, they had of Heidey with them and other company personnel, which had been taken in Japan, as well as a couple from Korea. On the back of each print, the captain wrote the names of the men in each photo with Heidey, along with the approximate date on which each photo was taken. These the captain put carefully into a small, ornamental album he bought at a Japanese shop in Yokohama, and gave to Heidey's parents.)

When the battalion emerged from the valley, there was not a man left in it who did not have at least a minor wound caused by a bullet, flying stone, steel, or wood, and received during one of the last days' battles.

Farther south, in the valley, the battalion found the road blocked by three burned US army trucks and an M-16. The battalion halted as the remaining Sherman tank made short work of ramming two of the burned trucks off the road and hauling the M-16 back farther to where it too could be shoved off the road.

The battalion then resumed its orderly retreat through the wide valley, by several small villages and frozen rice paddies, and on southward towards where its division's headquarters was last known to have been. None of the men had seen a Korean civilian since Thanksgiving Day. The only signs of life were smoke that sometimes drifted up from one of the huts they passed.

10

ROUT

By evening, the battalion camped on a gently-sloping, hillside field to the west of low hills. The road it had taken southward that day lay along the camp's eastern side. Despite its move southward, no contact had been made with its regimental headquarters or other divisional units.

The number of perimeter guards was almost doubled, and guards were posted in a number of outposts, outside the perimeter. The automatic weapons of both the inner and outer perimeters were positioned so fire from each foxhole could interlock with fire from the foxholes on each side of it. The men in the outposts were to identify approaching enemy and alarm the camp. Then they were to fall back to the outer perimeter—if possible.

Contact with regiment was re-established late that night. Col. McClusky's death was reported, and Capt. Wilson was ordered to serve as battalion commander. He, in turn, told Lt. Lauterbach to take command of Company B, and the lieutenant told Smith to command 1st Platoon and MacKenzie to serve as 2nd Platoon's commander.

Regiment told Capt. Wilson a defensive line was being prepared, mostly south of the Chongchon. What remained of battalion was to pass through this line and move to the rear.

The southward move continued along more winding valley roads, but there were no more skirmishes or battles with the Chinese. In fact, no one saw any Chinese during the remaining retreat. The infantrymen who could walked or rode the tank, for there was only enough room on the remaining trucks for the seriously wounded. The column moved on at a steady, but slow pace.

Along the road, the battalion lost another truck, which stopped with apparent engine trouble. It was shoved off the road and its engine blown up with a thermite grenade, which left it in flames. Slightly wounded infantrymen that had been on the tank now walked and were replaced on the tank by seriously wounded men, for whom there was no longer enough room on trucks and jeeps.

Eventually, the road led across the Taeryong River through more low hills, and then over the Chongchon River, near Sinanju. From there a road led, on the northern side of the Congchon, into the coastal road that led southward towards Pyongyang, the North Korean capital. By the time the battalion reached Sinanju, it had fewer vehicles, and some seriously wounded men walked, helped by more able-bodied GIs. Minor mechanical difficulties put the battalion's last Sherman tank out of commission, so its weapons were duly destroyed, and it was left by the roadside.

After a battle, GIs help a wounded comrade downhill to an aid station.

U.S. Army photo

Small arms, ammunition, and infantrymen's equipment were picked up along the road, which led by many apparently undamaged vehicles that appeared to need only fuel. Minor problems, like a flat tire, could be remedied by scavenging from a similar, abandoned vehicle. But the men had no tools with which to fix a tank and no way to siphon fuel from one vehicle for another. As a result, disabled vehicles were destroyed.

The battalion's strength was now about 400 men, including the seriously wounded. It had no armor, few trucks, and one jeep. Only the very seriously wounded rode. Except for drivers, the captain, and some wounded, all other men walked as best they could.

Capt. Wilson's jeep always had two seriously wounded men in the back seats. The men that could route-marched, two-abreast, in a column behind the jeep. At times, the captain got out and walked for a mile or two beside the men, to talk with them and encourage them. Whenever he did, he invited one of the walking wounded to take his seat in the jeep.

At Sinanju, the battalion reached the coastal road and was ordered to continue towards Pyongyang. By this time, it had no vehicles, and those wounded that could not walk were carried, or helped along, by other men. When it route-marched into the coastal road, several infantrymen were sent to stop traffic, and the battalion marched into the road and moved on southward.

Shortly after that, the rifleman behind MacKenzie said to him, "Hey Sarge, have you noticed how much company we have? Every mother's son from every other unit in the US Army in North Korea must be in this road with us, and some have no weapons."

Farther south, just north of Pyongyang, the road that led southwestward from Sunchon joined the road to Pyongyang. A few miles south of that junction, the road from the eastern coast entered the road to Pyongyang. By this time, the number of straggling soldiers and Korean refugees in the road to Pyongyang had reached flood proportions.

MacKenzie did not answer for a while, but eventually said, "I have noticed the only order the soldiers around our battalion seem to have is that privates straggle along with privates, noncoms with noncoms, officers with officers, and each nationality with men of the same nationality. Where are their units? What happened to their transportation, armor, artillery, and heavy weapons?"

Korean refugees were no longer in the road. They had been forced off and walked along or by railroad tracks to the west. The road was now filled mainly with US and Korean soldiers headed southward, but a noticeable number of men were from other nation's military units. Most were weaponless and without helmets. Many had even thrown away web belts, bayonets, canteens, mess kits, and other gear. They walked in small groups, with no order to them.

Mackenzie recognized unit identification badges of almost every nationality in the UN army. The only ones he could not see in the disordered, fleeing column were men of the Royal Ulster Rifles, the Scots, the English, or other units of the Commonwealth Division. He knew they had been headed to the Yalu also, and wondered what happened to them.

The rifleman behind MacKenzie said, "It looks as if half the US Army is here right now. You reckon these stragglers are from units we heard the Chinese smashed?

"It's the flotsam of regiments and divisions, for sure," said MacKenzie, "and your guess is as good a mine as to why their units broke and ran. You know we lost touch with our regiment and division. Well, that must have happened in spades across the front."

"A lot goes into causing something like this to happen," said Smith's familiar voice, over MacKenzie's shoulder. "The short explanation is lack of discipline, and control, and command. The longer answer also includes poor leadership, improper troop dispositions, bad communications, very bad intelligence, and top leaders that ignored intelligence that did not fit their plans. Add to that a mixture of unchecked rumor and panic and we have the scene we see around us.

"Almost every unit heard the rumors we heard and repeated and then believed them. They added to those rumors and passed them on, and instead of stopping the rumors, their officers began to believe them too. Then, when the panic began, the officers did nothing to stop it, because they were as spooked and panicked as the men they were supposed to discipline, command, and lead.

"I reckon this is the worst rout of the US Army since our grand daddies whipped it and routed it at First Manassas. It's as big a collapse as the French army's mutiny during World War I, or in 1940."

MacKenzie thought aloud, "When the French army collapsed, during the first world war, it stayed in the trenches. It just refused to attack. That's qualitatively different from this. Maybe this is like Carrhae, although the number of men involved in this rout is far greater."

"What is Carrhae?" asked one man.

"The battle at Carrhae was fought in 53 B.C. Carrhae was fought near the northern part of the Tigris River, in the northern part of a land named Parthia. The place of the battle is now part of Turkey. At that time seven Roman legions, with cavalry, had followed their Parthian enemy deep into a sandy desert. Near Carrhae they caught up to their enemy. The Romans learned much later the Parthians retreated to draw the Roman legions deeper into their own territory.

"The Romans outnumbered the Partians, but they faced an enemy that was mounted and mobile. The Parthians attacked with animal skins on their heads and arms and wild cries, as they banged hide-covered drums from which were hung bells and copper rings. The sound they made terrified the Romans momentarily.

115

"The Parthians had very strong bows and used camels to carry large supplies of arrows for their mounted bowmen. The Parthian's bows could fire an arrow through two Roman soldiers, which meant through two shields and the armor of two men. Because the bowmen were mounted, they were also very mobile. Anyway, they were able to kill many Legionaires from a distance that prevented the Romans from hurting them.

"The initial battle ended, but it was what the Parthians did next that made me think of Carrhae and this rout. At noon, they attacked again, and as they neared the Roman lines with drums, bells, and copper rings resounding, they unfurled banners that flashed in the sunlight and gleamed in a way no Roman there had seen before. The banners were made of very light, brightly colored material and embroidered with gold. They rose in the breeze and shone like fire and seemed to emanate power and invincibility.

"At that point, the formations of the surviving Legionaires' ranks, who suffered from thirst as well as from wounds, fell apart. The Roman soldiers fled in terror, at the awesome sight of silken banners shimmering and flapping in the breeze. About 20,000 Roman soldiers died there, and another 10,000 were taken prisoner."

Smith said, "Our divisions were fresh and neither thirsty nor wounded when they broke and fled. Our defeat seems to be completely psychological."

"Maybe so," said MacKenzie.

A statement by the soldier behind MacKenzie brought his thoughts back to the present: "If our great grand daddies had only followed the Yankees across the Potomac and taken Washington, D.C., we would be at home and not here."

The man beside him said, "If Pres. Davis had given Gen. Jackson the 10,000 men he asked for, he would have taken Washington and probably captured much of Lincoln's government. That would have ended the war."

"Was your great grand daddy in the Confederate army during Lincoln's War?" asked Smith.

"He surely was," said the soldier. "He was in a Kentucky regiment and fought through the whole war. He died of wounds he got defending Atlanta. His grave is there, with those of other good men that tried to defend the South's freedom. My daddy saw it, at Oakland Cemetery. And he saw the grave stone, with his name, state, and regimental number on it."

"My great grand uncle's body is buried there too," said Harrelson, who hailed from Columbia, Missouri. "He was with a Missouri regiment, but his body is in the mass grave where 500 bodies were buried that could not be identified individually. My daddy has a letter his company commander wrote after the war to those great grand parents, to tell them where their son had fallen and been buried."

"Well brothern," said Smith, "our forefathers did not chase the United States Army across the Potomac and end the war, so we are here on the farthest edge of US commitment trying to police this part of the world, and our only task for the moment is to maintain our military discipline and head to Pyongyang, or wherever else we are sent. So, stop crabbing and whistle Dixie. It will make y'all feel a lot better."

Smith gave the Kentuckian a friendly pat on the shoulder, and gave a thumbs up sign to the Missourian. Then he moved back to small talk again with men of another platoon to keep their moods up, in the midst of the unexpected military disaster they were caught up in.

"Harrelson, get with it, soldier," said a soldier two rows behind MacKenzie. "It does no good to think about what should have been done. We have a big, big problem right here, and if pigs could fly, pork prices would be lower."

"You're right," said Harrelson. "If ifs and ands were pots and pans, there would be no need for tinkers. All we can do is to have the same fighting spirit our blessed forebears had and try to keep the Chinese from kicking our butts. From what we see around us, what is left of our battalion may be the only unit in the US Army that is together and fighting fit."

"I don't reckon we're a fighting fit battalion," said another man. "We're the size of an over-strength company, and everyone of us has one or more wounds."

"You're right," said MacKenzie, "but even so, we may be the only battalion in the Eighth Army that has held together as a fighting force. At least we're the only one I've seen, so far.

"It shows how the war turned around. When we first landed in Korea, we were rushed northward to fight the North Korean army. The only thing most of us thought about was the pretty little Japanese girl, the 'jo san', we left behind. Then we met the North Korean army and had little time to think about anything else. They pounded us continually with massed frontal assaults supported by armor and artillery. Their leaders behaved the way Lincoln and Grant behaved.

They didn't care how many men they lost, if they could gain the objectives they wanted.

"The Chinese seem to be completely different. From what we have heard, I reckon many of their tactics are the kind Gen. Forrest would have approved. They know where we are and where we're headed. They infiltrate our lines and outflank us. They get between our units and catch us by surprise. And they attack at night to compensate for their lack of air cover, artillery, and armor. They lose a lot of men, but they have little fire power, unless they mass their soldiers.

"Our officers have had us to play the part played by the English and their British army troops during the French and Indian War, and the Chinese have been playing the part of the French and Indians. They stay off the roads and catch us in one ambush after another, because we are always on a road. They probably charge headlong into our guns when they reckon our guard is down, or their objective is so valuable the sacrifice will result in more victories later.

"When they attack and lose a thousand men, they cause severe damage to us. They may have millions of soldiers, but they may also be a lot less careless about their losses than were Lincoln and Grant, who didn't worry about losing 10,000 men in a charge, because they knew they had an almost endless supply of foreign immigrants and poor, drafted Yankees to fill their decimated regiments."

Turner, who hailed from Oklahoma, poked at MacKenzie's sleeve and said, "Look yonder! It looks as if every civilian in North Korea is headed south with us."

To the west, the men could see an unbroken column of civilians headed south. Most carried only what was on their backs and under their arms. A few had small carts with a few possessions on them.

"It's too bad Heidey caught it," the Oklahoman continued. "I'm willing to bet that there are many North Korean soldiers amongst those refugees, and no one bothers to screen any of them. There's no telling how many weapons and grenades there are under their clothing."

"There's no way we can screen them," said Darden. "We can't even hold our army together. What we need is someone to screen our side to find out why in hell we have been routed by an under-equipped army in rubber-soled, canvas tennis shoes."

"Lordy! Look yonder at Pyongyang," said a North Carolina soldier two men ahead of MacKenzie. "Look at that fire and smoke."

MacKenzie, and the men near enough to hear, looked towards Pyongyang. "My God, look at those columns of fire and smoke," said another man.

The ground shook, as if a minor earthquake had happened. In seconds, everyone headed southward walked with his eyes to the right, looking at the fire and columns of black smoke that cascaded skywards.

"Listen to those explosions," said another man. "Ammunition must be blowing up."

"Must be a lot of ammunition blowing up," said another man. "You reckon the Chinese air force attacked the supply dumps?"

"I reckon not," said Smith. "I have not seen a Chinese aircraft yet and never even saw a North Korean one over the Perimeter. I'd be willing to bet those fires and explosions were set by our men to keep the Chinese from getting the supplies and equipment. There is no unit effective enough to move it southward to where we might could use it. I also reckon those explosions mean we're headed for some point well south of Pyongyang."

"Damn!" said a man near him. "I'll bet our winter clothing is over there burning."

"Look at the bright side," said MacKenzie. "While we retreat, the Chinese may be slowed so much by the amount of supplies and equipment they capture, that we will have time to reorganize and whip them when we meet them the next time."

"I hope someone can do that damned quick, but I'd prefer to get the hell out of this country," said a man from California. "If I must fight, I'd prefer to do it for something that means a lot more to me than Korea."

11

HONORS

During a howling blizzard, the battalion crossed the frozen Imjin River and moved through a defensive line being prepared there. It moved on farther south to a rest area where the men showered, ate hot food, and slept under tents. They also received winter clothing and equipment, along with replacement personnel, which were integrated into the re-organized companies, along with new ordinance and vehicles.

After nearly two weeks in the rest area, Lt. Lauterbach told Smith to be certain he, MacKenzie, and Darden, the men who had attacked and destroyed a machine gun emplacement, were at the battalion's morning formation the next day, and not on guard duty. "Change the guard roster, if necessary," he told Smith.

The next day dawned cold and windy, and the battalion was ordered to fall in by company and platoon. Wind whipped snow against everything that was upright and, at times, limited the distance one could see. The men, nevertheless, noted the regimental commander, a brigadier general, and several members of his staff were present. After the usual formalities, Smith, MacKenzie, Darden and 28 other men were called forward. Then the battalion commander, Capt. Wilson, now Maj. Wilson, and aides walked down their rank and pinned on each a small, battle-blacked, metal emblem of the appropriate sergeant's rank each had been permanently promoted to.

After that, the officers and aides moved back to the rank's right side to where Smith, MacKenzie, and Darden stood. The general said to Smith, MacKenzie, and Darden, "I want to commend you each for your valor in action. It made me proud when I read the report of what you did. Your bravery in destroying a machine-gun nest and your subsequent, effective fire from the emplacement contributed significantly to your battalion's ability to defeat the enemy and move out of a dangerous situation with limited losses.

"Sgt. Smith, for your initiative and heroism, you have been awarded the Silver Star." To MacKenzie and Darden he said, "Each of you has been awarded the Bronze Star, for your heroism in helping to destroy the machine gun emplacement and subsequent effective fire on the enemy, from that position." This was the nearest the three could come to getting the actual medal in the field at this time, since none were actually being pinned on enlisted medal winners there in the field.

The final announcement was that Maj. Wilson would be transferred, effective immediately, to regimental staff, to serve as executive officer. His replacement as battalion commander would be

Lt. Col. Sturgis, a veteran with extensive combat experience in Europe during World War II. Other new officers were also announced.

Few men that had been sent to Korea in 1950 from garrison duty in Japan remained. Replacements included some men who had been wounded and were returning to duty, but more than 80 percent were new and without combat experience. More than 85 percent of the officers were new to the battalion. Few had combat experience, and every second lieutenant was fresh from officer's training in the States and without combat experience.

MacKenzie talked with the replacements in his squad and learned all were draftees, and none wanted to be in Korea. "Harris, what did you do before you were drafted?" he asked a man from Washington.

"I repaired typewriters and other office machines, and spent weekends fishing in the Snake River. It was a good life. My wife and I would pack the camping gear and some food and spend the weekend by the river for most of the year. I wish to hell I was back there now."

MacKenzie did not say it, but he knew Harris would do a lot of camping here.

There seemed to be a fair number of Southerners in the replacements received, but a lower percentage than in the professional army that had been sent from Japan when the war began, or amongst earlier replacements scavenged from army units in the States. These men were somewhat better educated, but clearly not from well-to-do families, and also not men who had enjoyed good educational opportunities.

12

RIDGWAY TAKES COMMAND

It was late January 1951 and Smith and MacKenzie were in a warming tent, with a dozen other men. MacKenzie was cleaning his rifle, while Smith read a letter. Several other men also cleaned their weapons, while the rest either played cards, wrote letters home, or enjoyed the warmth.

"My wife wants to know when I will be home," Smith said, looking up from a letter he had just written. "She reminded me my enlistment was up months ago, and said I should write my congressman and tell him to have the army discharge me."

"Fat chance," said MacKenzie, as he held his rifle up with the butt away from him, and tried to look down the barrel to see if it was clean. "Maybe your wife should go to see your congressman. She's pretty enough so he might would listen to her, just to see her smile."

"I wish it were that were doable," said Smith. "I wrote back and said to be patient. We are now south of the 38th Parallel and Seoul again and the new U.N commander, Gen. Ridgway, has been swift to rearrange the United Nations ground forces here. I like the changes and the way he enforces them. The men look a bit more orderly, for one thing. No more unbuttoned uniforms, for example. Our food is better, and our tactics are more attuned to the terrain."

"That's not what she wants to know, is it?" asked MacKenzie.

"No, but if the situation stabilizes, discharges may begin soon afterwards. I heard Ridgway has ordered the divisional commanders to get their men off the roads and to fight the Chinese where they are. When we move out we'll be expected to move out on foot and over the same terrain the Chinese move over. Our trucks will be for to carry in supplies and to carry out the wounded and dead. I reckon Ridgway's right. Now all we need is to know where the Chinese are.

"I understand he ordered tanks to be used to support infantry movements wherever possible. This is not tank-warfare terrain, but tank support for infantry is possible almost everywhere. That's the way Forrest used his cannon and the way US tanks were used in Europe in World War II.

"I reckon we are in better shape to fight now. This army feels a lot more like the army I was in during the last war. Ridgway has improved discipline and is here with us and not in Japan. He's had a good effect on morale, and I suspect there'll be no more panic. It also seems possible the army might just begin to discharge men whose enlistments have ended."

MacKenzie nodded and said, "He's replacing division commanders with younger men. He gives each one he replaces a Distinguished Service Cross and has him transferred stateside. That's one award higher than you got for risking your life, but who cares, if it gets rid of them."

"I've heard that too," said Smith. "I know we didn't know what ailed us, but I surely do reckon the men feel better for the changes. I know I feel we have a commander that does not hesitate to blame top brass when he thinks they are not fit for their commands. I reckon the army's fighting ability is much better now and it is probably a lot better led. We should be in pretty good fighting shape.

"I heard from the lieutenant that Ridgway ordered all field and company officers to get their men onto high ground and to position them appropriately for the terrain they are in. That means we must take tactically important positions.

"We can also expect visits from regimental and division commanders. Ridgway told them to visit the front and see the terrain we are on and what lies ahead. That's probably why our division commander was in our area yesterday. He was the first division commander in our area, since we arrived in Korea. I hope Ridgway forces the brass hats to be more responsible. Making them come to see the terrain we must fight on is a big step in the right direction, and I've heard positive comments from the men about that. I wonder how many mother's sons would be alive today, if Ridgway had been in command from the beginning?"

"Probably thousands," said MacKenzie. "When it comes to knowing terrain and making a secure camp, our battalion must be one of the few that has come close to following normal rules for camp-perimeter protection."

"True, but we did not have scouts out on every side to alert us to the enemy's presence and we rode along a valley floor and into every ambush."

The conversation between Smith and MacKenzie lapsed for a few minutes. Then Smith said, "You know, another bright spot, and a big one, is that we have been issued winter clothing we should have had two months ago. Here it is January, and the clothing has just been issued. If we had it two months ago, we would not have lost men because of frostbite."

"I wonder where the Chinese are," said MacKenzie. "The rumors I hear are that patrols sent northward have found very few in some areas and none in others. There seems to be at least a partial vacuum between us and the Chinese. I wonder if they are waiting to see what we do next, or if they have overextended their supply lines?"

"Be damned if I know," said Smith. "But no matter where they are, Ridgway has let it be known he reckons we can hold our own against the Chinese and that there is no need to evacuate our forces from Korea.

"But then, I heard he is taking no chances. I understand that, while he prepares us for combat, he has a lot of Koreans preparing a major defensive line in the southeast, around the old Pusan Perimeter. That must be just in case the Chinese smash through our lines again. We probably won't have to wait long to find out which way we are going to move."

"We're going to move out," said Lt. Lauterbach, now a captain and in command of Company B, as he briefed his platoon sergeants and squad leaders. "Our orders are to head northward again."

As the noncoms headed back to their platoons and squads, the man next to MacKenzie said sarcastically, "I'm delighted to be headed northward again, in this bone chilling weather.

"Well," MacKenzie said, "at least we are dressed better for it. Yet, low temperatures and wind seem to affect me worse than they did a few weeks ago. It's so damned cold, the moisture from our breath freezes on the hair in our nostrils, and vapor freezes on eyebrows and eyelashes. A machine-gun-crew member in 1st Platoon, touched his bare hand to a gun barrel yesterday, and the gunner had to cut parts of the man's fingers loose with a knife, before the whole hand froze.

The GI said, "My canteen is empty and I eat snow to get water. This would be a poor life for a dog."

"It could be worse?" one of the men said.

"How?" said MacKenzie.

"What if it was this cold and there was no snow?"

Beginning on January 25, 1951, the battalion was part of two divisions that moved northward, on part of a front. They met only occasional resistance from two Chinese armies. By February 9, the ruins of Suwon and Inchon were in allied hands.

"We are certainly on the way to Seoul again," said Smith, as he and MacKenzie walked through the ruins of Inchon and looked at the Yellow Sea, over the long mud flats exposed by the outgoing tide.

"What fantastic destruction," said MacKenzie. "I wonder if our next move will be into North Korea again?"

"No one seems to know," Smith said. "Just rumors and more rumors. But let's not worry about that now. It's time for chow. Let's get back and get some warm grub."

"Suits me," said MacKenzie. "I'm so hungry my belly thinks my throat is cut."

13

NIGHT ATTACK

"We've been ordered to move towards the central front to reinforce an area between here and the Taebaek Hills," Capt. Lauterbach told his noncoms. "Expect tough going, because this rainy weather has thawed the earth and made every road a mire."

"I'm glad to hear that," said one of the noncoms. "Otherwise I might have thought we had tough going up until now. I guess the really tough part is on the way. That'll learn me. See how easily a dog-face can be mistaken!"

The regiment moved towards the east. The men were on trucks, and the rest of the equipment was carried or drawn behind. The temperature had dropped, and the route led along what had been a road, but was covered with slippery ice. The temperature and wind made the air hurt and frostbite was as big a threat as the enemy. Eventually the regiment reached a place, on the central front, that was between two other US regiments. The vehicles drove northward for a short distance, and the infantry dismounted and moved onto the hills on each side of the vehicles. The infantry searched for Chinese, while the trucks lumbered slowly northward on the valley floor.

The landscape was barren, except for the scrubby bushes and stunted-looking trees that lined the lower slopes. Ahead, the land rose up to about 400 to 800 feet and then downwards another 400 to 800 feet. Climbing up and down was exhausting for men accustomed to riding to battle, but the GIs climbed up and down with fewer complaints than might have been expected. The main reason was that it took extra energy to complain, and few wanted to do that. As they climbed and descended, with shoulder weapons slung over a shoulder, they could not help wondering how many more ridges were ahead before they could form a perimeter and bed down for the night.

"Do these hills ever end?" a corporal asked MacKenzie.

"Not that I know, and these are only foothills. The big ones are ahead and east of us."

Before darkness fell, the regiment's battalions were abreast of each other and other regiments that now faced northward in a line across Korea.

"This is where we camp for the night," MacKenzie told the platoon's squad leaders. "Follow me and let me show you all where I want foxholes dug."

The squad leaders followed, and MacKenzie pointed out the vantage points where holes were to be dug and sentries posted. Occasionally, he ordered a bigger hole dug for a machine gun and its crew. Inside the battalion's perimeter were positioned mortars, howitzers, tanks, and tracked vehicles with dual mounted 40 cal. and quad-mounted 50 cal. automatic weapons.

At around midnight a sentry's shouts were heard, followed instantly by rifle and burp gun fire and the sound of shouts, bugles, horns, and grenades. The platoon's members slept with their sleeping bags unzipped, and were, as a result, on their feet, rifles in hands, in seconds. MacKenzie shouted to his squad leaders to form a skirmish line and move towards the noise. The adrenaline-filled riflemen fixed their bayonets as they moved.

Before the 2nd Platoon's GIs had gone 150 feet towards the noise, the Chinese noisemakers charged into them. They were armed with rifles, percussion grenades, or satchel charges. The GIs began to shoot at the Chinese, and some Chinese shot back. Those that survived the GIs' fire tried to swarm through the platoon and on into the inner perimeter, like angry bees followed by a tall Chinese armed with a pistol and grenade.

GIs and Chinese tangled in hand to hand combat, killing with rifle butts and bayonets. Other GIs turned to fire at Chinese who had run through them. They steadied their rifles and shot as quickly as they could aim. The 15 to 20 surviving Chinese headed towards the tanks and tracked vehicles which were often used with deadly effect on Chinese infantry.

When they neared a Patton tank parked nearest the 2nd Platoon, several GIs came from behind the vehicle and fired from about 30 feet away, killing the leader and most of the men, including two with satchel charges. Five Chinese were taken prisoner.

"We done good," one rifleman said, as he walked back over the ground the swift infiltration had covered. It was strewn with at least 135 dead, dying, or seriously wounded Chinese. Outside the unit's perimeter were about 100 more Chinese dead and several critically wounded ones. The 2nd Platoon had lost its new second lieutenant, a man named Burke, as well as three enlisted men killed, and 10 wounded. Altogether, the company had lost seven dead and 24 wounded. The wounded were gathered near the perimeter's southern side, for movement to a field hospital.

As MacKenzie walked over the ground the battle had raged on, he heard his name said by a clear, but low voice. He stopped and looked towards where he thought the voice came from and saw an arm raised by a body lying on its side a dozen feet away. He walked over, knelt by the man, and saw he was trying to turn himself onto his back. MacKenzie helped him into that position.

"What happened, Connor?" MacKenzie asked.

"I was hit by something, as they came towards us. I fired and dropped two. Then I was hit. I felt the impact: a hot searing feeling, as I fell. Then, after a minute, the pain began. I can't feel my legs. I know I ain't going back to Arkansas. This is taps for me."

"Don't give up, Connor. A medic should be here in a few minutes."

But MacKenzie knew differently, for he saw Connor's innards were torn up and partly outside his body. He scanned the battlefield for a medic and, when he saw one, raised his arm high and hollered, "Medic! Over here!"

"I'm ready for to cross the river," said Connor, "can you re-baptize?"

"I surely can," said MacKenzie, who used a bit of snow as water, as he recited a Baptist-like prayer appropriate for a re-baptism, as best he could recall it.

"This snow will have to do. We have no river or lake, and dunking anyone in one would freeze the person baptized stiff in a minute," he said with as much of a smile as he could manage.

Connor managed a slight grin, as he gritted his teeth against pain.

"Let me see," said a voice beside them.

MacKenzie looked up and saw a medic, who quickly bent, cut open the trouser over Connor's left leg and, taking a morphine ampule from his mouth, where he kept ampules to keep them from freezing, put it into a syringe and injected it into Connor. Then he tied a tag to Connor to show the amount of morphine given and when given.

"What is heaven like, do you think?" asked Connor.

"I reckon when one crosses the river it is right nice there. Green and wooded, with pleasant breezes and clear, fresh rivers, creeks and runs, and mile of elbow room on every side."

"And the Lord?" asked Connor.

"He's watching over his flock. I reckon heaven is a pleasant place for to spend eternity. It's a place to be with God. The soul that comes there can look for kin that have already passed on in the Lord and can wait for those that are acoming."

"Yes," said Connor. Then his body went limp, although his eyes remained half opened.

The medic felt for a pulse and then said quietly, "He passed." He got up and quietly moved on to find another wounded man to treat.

MacKenzie closed Connor's eyelids. As he lifted his rifle from his knee and placed the butt on the ground preparatory to standing, he heard, at his elbow, "You did well. I don't think a chaplain could have given more comfort to a dying man than you just did."

It was Capt. Lauterbach, who, from a few feet away, had watched as MacKenzie ministered to Connor. MacKenzie stood up facing the captain, who put his gloved hand on MacKenzie's shoulder and patted it several times silently. Then the captain turned and continued to survey the carnage.

Capt. Lauterbach shared with several of his noncoms what he had seen and heard when MacKenzie ministered to Connor. The information about MacKenzie and Connor gradually spread through most of the company, and then battalion, and lost nothing in the telling. MacKenzie quickly, and unbeknownst to him, gained an aura of specialness in the minds of many of the men. He gradually became aware of this, as men from other platoons came to talk about a troubling letter from a fiancée, girl friend, or wife, or financial problems a wife or parent had, and other similar problems.

MacKenzie listened and managed to make each man feel comfortable, although they held a variety of religious beliefs and came with a variety of problems. He tried to understand each man's problem and give general advice that would not harm, even if he could not always set a man's mind fully at ease. He hoped just listening carefully to them was helpful.

Behind his back, some men called him "the chaplain" and others "the fightin' skypilot," not in mockery or fun, but as a mark of special respect they had for a comrade in arms who fought beside them to kill the enemy and could counsel them to comfort their minds and souls.

14

OUTFLANKING

During February, the weather was unseasonably cold and wet. The icy cold rain that first pelted the poncho-covered troops did not ease. It was months too early, and MacKenzie began to wonder about the accuracy of the *Guide to Korea* he had bought in Japan.

The icy pelting continued both day and night. Snow and ice melted and ground thawed. Dirt roads that had been usable by trucks turned into muddy tracks, difficult to drive a truck or jeep over. It was a challenge to drive vehicles in these tracks, and for those men that had to move on foot, the mud was worse. They sank into it up to their ankles and sometimes higher. It held fast to their boots and made movement difficult and wearisome.

The battalion was moved, with the regiment, into reserve and to a rest area not many miles behind the UN line. It had received replacement officers and men in ones and twos, for several weeks. In reserve, it received more and had a short time to try to weave them into the battalion's fiber. The men also showered, were given clean clothes, and enjoyed hot meals each day.

That was when Rigmer returned to the company, after temporary duty at battalion headquarters. He told about an errand he did for battalion to division headquarters, in terms that might have been similar to the way in which someone that had never been out of prairie cornfields might tell about a visit to a middling-sized metropolis.

"I come from a town of nearly 4,000 people," he said, "but division headquarters looks bigger. It must be 12 miles south of our position, where it spreads from one side to the other of a wide valley and stretches as far south as I could see. It's a town of tents, as well as a few buildings that must have been part of a Koran town, maybe a town hall, a school, and another permanent structure.

"I was driver for Lt. Schutzmann, one of the lieutenants at battalion, and drove us towards the place from higher ground. As we came over a rise in the road and drove downhill towards it, I tried to do a quick estimate of the number of tents and drive at the same time. I counted at least 200 tents before we reached lower ground, and I lost an overview of the metropolis.

"The lieutenant got out at the main building and I waited outside, in the jeep. When he was through with his business, he sent me, with one of the headquarters clerks, to the enlisted men's chow tent and went off to eat in the officers' mess.

"When we came inside the chow tent, the clerk and I each picked up a metal tray and got into the line formed to get chow. Once we had knives, forks, spoons, and food on our trays we walked into the next tent and seated ourselves on a bench by a table, put our trays onto the table, and ate.

"The food was hot and tasted wonderful. So did the coffee. I thought: this is the life! Hot food every day! The nearest these men come to war is a river of reports about it that stream in continually from combat units.

"After we ate, I went back to the office with the clerk to wait for my lieutenant. He came in, about two hours later, and we headed back to battalion. On the way, he told me a little of what he had seen, after he ate chow. It seems he was there to check the status of a man from battalion that was charged with desertion.

"He said he visited the soldier in a detention tent. The tent the man was in had only eight cots in it, with a foot locker for each cot. Four of the cots were unoccupied. He said three of the men, including the one from our battalion, were awaiting trial for desertion and the fourth for deliberately wounding a sergeant while attempting to kill him. Not good company, he said.

"I wondered about the desertion charges, since so many troops threw away their weapons and ran, when the Chinese came into the war. I could only think enforcement of discipline has changed, since Ridgway took command.

"I remember, after we landed at Inchon, when the lieutenant that commanded this platoon, was ordered to take a fortified hill position near Inchon. The fortified position was a fortress called the Citadel. This story is true. I'm not shitting you all. Smith and MacKenzie were there too and will remember what happened.

"The lieutenant told the company commander the order was suicidal and refused to lead an attack. He soon reported he had accidentally broken his glasses and said he could not see to lead the troops. The battalion commander was furious and told him to feel his way up the hill, but thought better of it and replaced him.

"The replacement, another first lieutenant, listened to the order. Then he went back to his tent and shot off one of his toes. He was replaced by a barrel-chested second lieutenant, from Georgia, who stood about 5 feet 9 inches tall. His name was McBride, and he was also ordered to lead the platoon and take the Citadel. He came to us and told us exactly what we had to do and what he expected the North Koreans to do to stop us. He said we would have a hard fight, and then he deployed us and led us up that hill. We took the Citadel and lost many dead and wounded taking it. But we took it!

"I wondered what was done to the second lieutenants that refused to fight. I never found out.

"While I was at division and waiting for the lieutenant, I saw a soldier named Greenspan. He's a draftee, from Baltimore. I remembered the day, shortly after Ridgway took command, when our battalion was issued extra ammunition and rations and told we would attack early the next morning. Greenspan was one of several replacements that had arrived in our unit only a week earlier. When he heard we were to prepare to attack the next day, he whimpered and said he could not. He demanded to see a chaplain of his faith. They probably had to let him, so he was sent back to division to see his chaplain. While he was on his way to division, we attacked and took a lot of casualties.

"Shortly after that we learned Greenspan had been relieved of his duties with battalion and transferred out. Until I met him at division, I didn't know he had been transferred to it. Turns out he was assigned to the commanding general's honor guard. I asked him if it was not cowardly to avoid his duty, and he laughed and said he would rather be a live coward than a dead hero.

"As the lieutenant and I drove back we talked about the Citadel, the lieutenants that refused to fight, and the mass desertions when the Chinese attacked. We talked about Greenspan, and the lieutenant agreed it is unfair that some men are ordered to serve or fight and most others left alone in civilian life or allowed to shirk. We talked about the men in the detention tent charged with desertion and about the amount of desertion that had happened before Ridgway arrived, and the fact we never heard of any courts-martial for them. We reckon the men at division that are charged with desertion must be the result of Ridgway's enforcing military discipline."

Desibeau, one of the riflemen listening said, "Yeah, whatever they did, I feel sorry for 'em. If the military has decided to enforce the rules and has one shred of evidence they might be guilty, they are in real trouble."

"You bet 'cha! said Chastain, who had also been listening. "You know the rule for military courts-martial of enlisted men is, 'Bring the guilty bastard in, and we'll give him a fair trial before we hang him.'' Those men aren't in the officers' fraternity. There's no one will twist his vote, on a court-martial board, to save their butts the way they will for a brother officer.'"

"Shit," said DeMott, another rifleman, "an officer would have to be guilty of a crime witnessed by hundreds, before any formal discipline would happen. Even then, it would probably take pressure from the press to make it happen."

After two weeks in reserve, the regiment was returned northward to the main UN line. Several days later, the battalion was ordered to patrol several miles north of the line to try to contact the enemy.

They advanced, by road, in trucks, with two tanks in the lead, across low-lying hills and through a deserted, half-destroyed village where two dirt roads crossed. As they advanced farther northward, they heard a whistle blow and machine guns began to fire at them from a hill to the northeast, and mortar rounds began to explode and splatter steel splinters, stone, and dirt through the air around them.

The riflemen hastily dismounted and took what cover they could behind bushes, scrub pines, small boulders, and tanks. The initial firing wounded several GIs and killed one.

The Chinese force seemed not to be as large as Company B, but Capt. Lauterbach preferred to destroy it with napalm and cannon fire from the air force and called battalion and asked for an air strike. The request was relayed up the command chain, but word came back that the air force was busy elsewhere and no tactical support would be available here. Despite that, the company was ordered to engage the Chinese and determine their strength.

The lieutenant in command of 1st Platoon, called for two tanks to move forward. From behind each tank, an infantryman directed the tank's canon to fire at suspected Chinese positions.

A Chinese machine gun was dug in high up the hill's stony incline. It was supported by riflemen in well-dug foxholes and by two or more light mortars behind the hill's crest, which lobbed rounds into and around Company B. The Chinese riflemen were well concealed behind dirt and stone heaped in front of their foxholes and screened partly by bushes and trees.

The platoons were quickly organized and the men ordered to spread out off the road, on the hill-slope to the west of and facing the Chinese positions. MacKenzie sized up the situation and crawled over to talk with Lt. Bain, who now commanded 2nd Platoon.

"We cannot stay here and wait for the tanks to clean up the Chinese. Let me take two squads over the slope to our left and move to the north and then come back over behind that hill.

"We have not been fired on from the western side of the hill. I reckon we have run into a small number of Chinese placed here as a trip wire to warn of our approach. Their rear is probably not well defended. We might could get behind that hill and come up over it onto this side and shoot down into them. From where we are now, we can only take the hill by advancing frontally. Let me try this, before we are all hamburger meat."

"Good!" said Lt. Bain. "I'll suggest that to the company commander."

Capt. Lauterbach was reached by radio and accepted the suggestion. Lt. Bain told MacKenzie to choose his squads and move out. "We will pin them in their positions, while you come in behind them. When you reach the top call me on a walkie-talkie and let me know. We will adjust our fire to keep it below you and your men. If you run into trouble, withdraw. Good luck, sergeant."

"Thanks, sir," said MacKenzie, and then crawled back, over the stony ground towards roadside bushes. His platoon's four squads were at full strength, except for one man that had been wounded in the initial ambush. MacKenzie wanted the 1st and 2nd squads with him on this venture. Second squad was formerly MacKenzie's, and Darden was now its leading noncom and the most competent and reliable man MacKenzie knew in the company.

When he had crawled up the slope a few yards, MacKenzie rose and ran, hunched over to keep a lower profile, to where the squads awaited him. He called the squad leaders to him and told them what he planned. With great emphasis, he said, "Remember: we want to surprise them, so, there must be complete silence, at all times, until the fighting begins. If we reach the area behind the hill yonder undetected, be sure no one makes any noise, or we might be the ones surprised and killed."

The squads MacKenzie commanded were fairly well hidden by bushes and small trees, on the low hill's lower slope. He led the two squads, 25 men in all, up the slope and away from the valley. They reached the ridge, south of where the rest of the company was, undetected. When they reached the crest, they lay down and crawled over it and down to a point where they could stand and not be seen by anyone on the other side.

They then moved northward, single file, through the somewhat protective cover of bushes and small trees. The battle's sound grew more muffled as they moved north of the Chinese-held hill. MacKenzie climbed to the crest, crawling the last few yards to it, and looked over at the battle area. Then he led the squads another 500 yards to the north, where they climbed to the crest and crawled over it and down to where they could carefully move down the hill using trees and bushes for cover.

Once in the valley again, they moved eastward and over the hill directly north of the one the Chinese were dug in on. The noise of the battle was now quite clear. Then, they crossed the hill and moved southward onto the one the enemy held.

They saw no Chinese, but the hill rose, with a hump between where they were and the crest. The Chinese mortar crews were sited there and the machine gunners and riflemen on the other side.

They encountered no enemy on their way up the hill, until they reached a point about 200 ft. below the crest. There they were spotted by several Chinese soldiers who were probably with two mortar crews sited only a few feet below the crest. Several Chinese soldiers fired at them with no effect, and GIs shot them down and continued to move to the crest. Before they reached it, they overran two mortar emplacements and silenced them permanently.

MacKenzie called Lt. Bain on his walkie-talkie. He reported the squads' location and that they would move over the crest in four minutes. The lieutenant relayed this information to the GIs on the valley floor, including the tankers, and fire was then concentrated on the lower 150 feet of the almost 400-foot-high hill.

Company B's fire did no harm to MacKenzie and his command as they started down the hillside facing Company B, but it did little harm to the Chinese either. However, it kept the Chinese occupied and their attention directed to the GIs in the valley.

As MacKenzie moved down the hill a little ahead of the squads, Darden was within two yards of him. The squads encountered several Chinese soldiers entrenched there and, in a succession of firefights, killed them with rifle fire. From that point, they shot into several deep foxholes manned by Chinese. When targets ducked, they tossed fragmentation grenades into the holes.

Less than a third of the way down, MacKenzie and Darden saw firing coming from a very well camouflaged bunker. They moved down to a point above it and tossed a grenade into the bunker. The grenade exploded and set off a secondary explosion, which caused the bunker's roof to rise, as if an earthquake shook it, and knocked both MacKenzie and Darden to the ground.

Both men were on their feet in a few seconds and entered the bunker. They found there was a tunnel in the back and followed it for about 20 feet, to where it turned towards the hillside. There they came in behind Chinese manning a machine gun. MacKenzie tossed in a grenade, which exploded. The machine gun was silent and MacKenzie heard no sounds, so he entered the bunker slowly.

He saw a Chinese soldier's bloody body sprawled on the ground facing the hillside and another lying bloodied and still against the bunker's wall farther to the right. He was just a foot into the bunker when another Chinese body, lying near his feet, turned over and raised his right hand, with a pistol in it. Darden saw the pistol an instant before MacKenzie and jumped forward, with his rifle leveled at the man, to a position on MacKenzie's left. As he did this, the Chinese moved his hand towards Darden, and MacKenzie and the Chinese fired at the same time.

Darden's body was thrust back against the tunnel's wall by the bullet's impact, which went through his right lung and out his back. MacKenzie fired two more rounds into the Chinese and then pulled Darden onto the bunker floor. He propped his head up, and then quickly joined the squads, which had now moved several yards below the bunkers.

The tanks and GIs, on the valley floor, had stopped firing at the hill, and only an infrequent rifle shot came from the remaining Chinese. The hill was not as fortified as the men of Company B thought, but the remaining Chinese, now completely on the defensive, fought back tenaciously and died bravely. None tried to surrender.

As soon as the last Chinese had been killed, MacKenzie called on the walkie talkie for medics, and told four GIs to follow him. He returned to the bunker where Darden lay. He had not stayed with Darden, for wounded men were supposed to be tended only by medics. Now, with fighting over, he returned to where Darden lay.

He lifted Darden's head and shoulders in a futile attempt to make him more comfortable. Darden's uniform was covered with blood where the bullet had torn a hole in his chest. The ground under him was also awash in his blood. Darden was ashen grey and clearly dying quickly. MacKenzie could hear the sound of air being sucked into the wounded lung, with every terribly painful breath Darden took.

Bloody spittle trickled from the side of his mouth, a certain sign of a deadly wound when far from medical help.

Darden's eyes showed life was ebbing from him, and he said weakly, "I did my best, Mac. Now I won't be able to pay you what I owe."

"You saved my life. Don't worry about money," MacKenzie said. "It's only for spending. I radioed for medics and a way to get you to a field hospital."

"Medics can't do no good for me," Darden said. "I bought one and its check-out time. I'm going home. Will you write to my folks and tell them how I died? Their address is on the envelope of a letter in my pack."

"I promise I will," said MacKenzie.

MacKenzie had the GIs with him lift Darden and carry him out onto the hillside where MacKenzie called to Rodriquez, the 1st Squad's corporal, and told him to send a runner to get the medics to Darden, as soon as they arrived.

By the time a medic reached them, Darden was mercifully unconscious. The medic gave Darden a shot of morphine, and then the GIs carried the limp body a distance behind the company, where he was strapped to a stretcher secured over the back seats of a jeep. He was carried back to a field hospital were there were doctors, blood for transfusions, and other medical supplies and equipment.

The battle, or skirmish, depending upon one's viewpoint, ended nearly five hours after it began. Company B had lost three men dead and 12 wounded, thanks only to the Chinese riflemen's notoriously poor aim. Forty-five dead Chinese were counted and two light mortars and two light machine guns were destroyed on the hill. With that light compliment, the ambushers were clearly not there to do more than slow the UN and enable a warning about the UN advance to be sent to their headquarters.

Capt. Lauterbach reported the skirmish and its results to battalion and was told Company B should now withdraw southward, along the same route it had taken earlier that day, and return to the regiment's positions.

By the time the company returned to the regiment's positions, Darden was dead.

15

NORTHWARD

The next evening, battalion received an order to move ahead six miles to a small village where an east-west road crossed the north-south road it moved along. Its assignment was to determine if the enemy had a force in the village and, if the force was small, destroy it and hold the position. If it was large, it was to withdraw southward back to the line now held.

At dawn the next day, Company B, riding on tanks, moved northward in the lead, and the rest of the battalion followed with the battalion's vehicles. On the way, they neither saw nor heard an enemy, until they were within a mile of the village. At that point, several snipers fired at them, and they returned fire in the enemy's general direction with rifles and the tanks' machine guns. On the two occasions when they were able to spot exactly where the snipers were, the lead tank's main gun was fired at the luckless enemy sending part of low hillsides flying into the air in bits and pieces.

When they reached the village, enemy fire increased, and the tanks fired at every humble farm hut that might have concealed an enemy, causing parts of walls and roofs to fly in every direction.

Company B had slid off the tanks and moved into the village, alongside and behind the tanks. It moved towards the remaining huts to search them, but was fired on and returned fire, along with the tanks' main guns. The noise and bright flashes of tank rounds exploding and huts being destroyed rent the air and blended with the crackling sound of the wooden buildings burning, while smoke billowed up and out and layered over the scene of destruction. Huts collapsed and spewed sparks, smoke, rubble, and intense heat upwards and outwards from the falling walls and roofs.

When it was over, Capt.. Lauterbach said he reckoned they had disturbed a small Chinese unit of about 15 to 20 men, which had been placed there to delay them while most of their comrades escaped. After the place had been secured, the battalion moved in and began to set up a defensive line facing northward.

"Why are we stopping here for the night, Sarge?" a rifleman asked MacKenzie.

"Reckon there's a reason. The order is to dig in for the night, so we can defend ourselves. Large Chinese units have been sighted headed our way."

Other US and allied units had scouted areas north, west, and east of the battalion and had found no enemy, or only small outposts placed so as to provide the Chinese with warnings, if the UN forces moved northward. On the next day, the rest of the UN's line units moved northward to positions flanking the battalion and prepared defensive positions that gave each unit the ability to maintain physical contact with those on its flanks.

Capt. Lauterbach's breath froze so quickly that a frosty mist was in front of his face and nearly hid him. He walked quickly over to Smith and said, "Smith, you see the terrain ahead of us to the left? You and your platoon get rolls of barbed wire from a vehicle and string two strands of it along an east-west line, about 500 feet from the slope's bottom. When you meet the wire of the platoons to your left and right, you will know you all have completed the forward line. At that time, you must move back up the slope about 600 feet and string two more wires in both directions and connect with the wires being strung on each side of us.

"Once y'all have done that, dig in anti-personnel mines in the areas marked by the engineers, and then rig mines along the outer sides of the inner and outer defense lines. Stay within the engineers' markings. Rig the mines to explode, if a wire is moved hard enough. The last step will be to get half-full barrels of gasoline from the rear area, and roll them along the outer and inner lines. Then connect each one to a trip wire, so each will explode when someone touches it.

"Bury one anti-personnel mine for every 10-yards of terrain, beginning 50 feet outside the outer perimeter wires and continuing to the wires along the inner perimeter. The units on each side will do the same thing in their sectors. We are supposed to leave a 10-feet-wide path between companies, and the same between platoons. I also want foxholes dug every 200 feet, in the area between the outer and inner wires, with 30 feet clear on all sides of each hole.

"In the mined and unmined areas outside the outer wires, rig trip flares about 15 feet apart. I'll be here to see the machine gun crews and BAR teams place their foxholes in positions that reinforce the riflemen and give us interlocking fire fields. When you all are through placing mines, come inside the outer wires and dig foxholes to support the machine guns and BARs. Use the dirt and stone from each hole to make a semi-circular berm, in front and on both sides of each position."

"Yes, sir, captain," said Smith, and waved to his squad leaders to come to him. At his order, the platoon followed him to the trucks to get barbed wire rolls.

The defensive lines were soon prepared and, inside the inner one, machine guns and BARs were also sited. Behind them, tracked vehicles and tanks were positioned in readiness for an attack. Farther back, behind the battalion, mortar positions were dug and mortar crews readied their positions for action.

At two in the morning, with their usual noise, the Chinese attacked 2nd Platoon's position in battalion strength. Mines exploded and flares lit the area, as Chinese tripped over wires that fired them. Mortar rounds also exploded here and there in the GIs' positions, but the GIs saw clearly where the Chinese were before they reached the first barbed wire, and US mortar rounds exploded amongst them and GIs fired their rifles into their attackers' ranks, while machine guns, BARs, and especially anti-aircraft guns, shredded many. Only a few Chinese were visible by the outer wires, and their bodies hung limply on then. The few surviving Chinese retreated back into darkness.

About half an hour later, mortar rounds again fell amongst the GIs' positions, and what appeared to be an even larger number of Chinese soldiers swarmed out of the darkness, accompanied by the din of shepherds' horns, bugles, whistles, and shouts that would have been hard to understand, even if yelled in English, because of the din the attackers made.

The onrushing Chinese charged ahead towards the outer barbed wire and were cut down by heavy fire from rifles, machine guns, BARs, and tank and anti-aircraft guns. They suffered frightful losses, but the mass of Chinese soldiers continued to press onwards to the accompaniment of exploding land mines and mortar rounds in their midst and the concentrated fire of every weapon the platoons had. They breached the first line of barbed wire, and many more were shot down or were blown backward by explosions, cannon or anti-aircraft gunfire.

Some fell in rows where machine gun or BAR fire had cut them down. In some instances, body parts flew into the air in every direction. Where a Chinese soldier stepped on a mine, his partly dismembered body was flung several feet into the air and men around him were wounded or killed.

Despite this, hundreds of surviving Chinese rushed ahead, exploding mines and gasoline barrels and setting off flares. Their losses, just to get inside the outer wires, were great. Nevertheless, the survivors pressed forward, propelled by the pressure of men behind them.

When the Chinese breached the first wires, surviving US riflemen outside the inner wires fell back in disarray in a race to get inside the inner wires, before the Chinese overran them or cut them down. As they did, mortar rounds exploded in the area between the inner and outer wires and machine guns, BARs, and tank and anti-aircraft guns roared death into the charging ranks.

In addition, a 75 mm pack howitzer had been hauled from behind the line and dug into a position behind the inner wires. Its towing end was raised high by putting dirt and stones under it, and its crew was able to it aim its muzzle in a trajectory level with the ground before it. After the Chinese breached the outer wires, the crew fired at them. Each round fired was phosphorous and, in a blazing burst of light, appeared to shred one or two dozen bodies and send their parts swirling into the air, in all directions.

The noise level was high as men shouted and screamed in pain, while weapons fired and gasoline barrels and mines added their explosions and thunder to the hell-like scene and sounds that spread carnage across the battle field. No individual command could be heard from more than three feet away.

When the Chinese reached the inner-wire line, its leaders had been shot down or blown to pieces, and the attackers seemed to stop. Then some of them breached the wires, while others, farther away, began to move somewhat aimlessly, and then retreated into the darkness.

More than 50 Chinese had gotten inside the inner wires, despite the deadly effect the steel hail storm had had on their unit. Most were killed by rifle fire or with bayonets Three unwounded Chinese surrendered. They appeared to have charged without any weapons.

The battlefield was now relatively quiet. The only noise was the sound of wounded men moaning or screaming in pain. Medical personnel gathered up wounded GIs and Chinese from within the barbed wire lines, as well as the bodies of dead GIs. After initial treatment where they fell, the wounded were moved to safer positions near the mortar emplacements, behind the battalion's positions. There they awaited transport to a field hospital.

The GIs worked swiftly, in frigid, windy weather that stung the skin, to repair the barbed-wire lines and set new mines, flares, and gasoline barrels linked to trip wires. Within an hour they had completed some of these tasks and strung new wire where the outer wires had been breeched. They were at work on the area between the outer and inner wires when another large Chinese unit made a frontal assault on their position. There was no way to tell the number of Chinese attacking, but there appeared to be about 1,000.

This time, despite huge losses, the Chinese quickly breached the outer wires and ran on towards the inner ones. Behind them there were isolated islands of GIs killing every Chinese they could and hoping they would not be killed by the friendly fire now whizzing by, exploding nearby, and raining down from above.

At the inner wires, the Chinese charge staggered to a stop, in the face of the US firepower, which thinned their ranks second by second. Then, once again, the Chinese retreated, continuing to lose men at every step, as they ran back through the breeched outer wires and into the night's shielding darkness.

Medical personnel moved again across the battlefield treating and gathering the wounded and bearing off dead GIs. The platoon, and those on each side of it, which had supported it during the battles, sent men behind their lines for more ammunition.

A medic gives first aid to a fallen GI, as combat continues around them.
U.S. Army photo

As Smith approached a 30-cal. machine gun crew inside the inner wire lines, the GI in charge of it was cursing roundly.

"What's the matter?" Smith asked, as he strode up to the crew's foxhole.

"We burned out the damned barrel," answered the GI.

"I'll see what I can do to remedy that," Smith said. In a foxhole inside the outer wires, he found a BAR and rifle that had been used by the now dead GIs that had been there. These he carried back and gave to the machine gun crew. He then posted them in an empty foxhole, inside the outer wire, and sent one man back for ammunition.

Smith had other men from 1st Platoon take positions just vacated by the machine gun crew. Then he sent men for a supply of grenades and distributed these to the men, so each had two.

As the battlefield held by Company B became quieter, the men gradually became aware of a great din on the regiment's right flank. In addition to the noise, the sky over the noise was lit by flares, which gave notice that a major battle raged there.

Capt. Lauterbach strode up to Smith and said, "The main Chinese attack came to the east, where our regiment's line meets the next regiment's. The Chinese breeched the line at that point and a large number of them moved through and turned our flank. The colonel wants Company B to move back to protect the flank and send out patrols to find and kill infiltrators. We're being relieved here by a company from the regimental reserve."

Early that morning, as the reserve company moved into Company B's positions to take over, the soldier from Oklahoma in MacKenzie's platoon looked at one of them and said "Welcome sunbeams! Ya'll are taking over some of the finest vacation land in Korea. Ya'll are no doubt familiar with drive-in theaters. Well, this here terrain is like that, but it's a run-in theater and live, night action is the usual feature. Why, we've just been through a very exciting triple feature that used real killers."

"It's not funny," said the nearest replacement, a New Yorker, who spit to the side to emphasize his lack of empathy with the other's humor.

GIs rest, after beating off a night-long Chinese attack.

U.S. Army photo

"Did you tell the main desk to have the towels and bed linen changed?" said another Company-B rifleman. The New Yorker winced, made an inaudible response, and kept moving. His mumbling was evident only because his lips moved and the volume of freezing breath that flowed from his mouth increased noticeably.

On the next morning, an angry, orange-colored sun rose over the eastern hills, giving no warmth to those under it. The company, which was camped a short distance behind the battalion's line, readied itself for the day's work. Then the order, "Company B, fall in!" was shouted loudly, and the men moved rapidly to obey. After a weapons inspection, the company moved, in a single file, farther south from the battalion's line. They walked along fairly level terrain for about two miles and then walked up from the low ground and onto the hill to their east. From there, they walked up and down hills and looked for any telltale sign of Chinese troops suspected of being in the area.

It was almost dark by the time they camped on a low hill and dug a defense ring of foxholes for sentries around it. Each day they searched and each evening they camped.

"My legs are ruined," a GI said to MacKenzie. "I don't think I can climb another hill. Every muscle hurts so it's painful to lift the legs."

"Think about the Chinese! They walk like this every time they move. We're just not used to it," said MacKenzie. "I know I feel weary from all the walking up and down hills that we've done."

"They're used to it," the soldier said. "This is more marching and harder marching than I ever did, even in recruit training."

"Think how physically well conditioned you'll be, when this is over," said another man.

"Hell! This will never be over, and what makes you think we'll get out of this in one piece, or even alive!"

GIs watch smoke from a phosphorus-shell explosion drift towards them, as they walk in a strung-out file from the hill's far side and up towards another hill top.

U.S. Army photo

"Reckon it will end eventually, but there's no telling where we'll be by then."

"Can you men think about something nicer," said MacKenzie. "Think about the girls you left behind and what it will be like to get back to them."

The man answered, "I'll need a two-week-long bath, before any of them will let me get near them. I'm crusted with dirt and my clothes have bonded to my body."

"Where are the Chinese?" said another man.

"If there are Chinese in this area, they are well hidden," a corporal said to MacKenzie. "We were told they came through this way, but we haven't even found a trace of them."

"I've seen nothing to indicate Chinese in the area," said MacKenzie. "If they came through here, they covered their tracks well and are too smart and careful to throw away anything that would show they were here. We should have seen prints of their tennis shoes when we went over damp ground, but we've seen none." The corporal said, "The Chinese may have moved farther south and out of the area we searched. Or they may have taken cover and watched us search for them."

"Both situations are possible," said MacKenzie.

After several days of fruitless searching, the weary GIs returned to their battalion.

16

CHANGES

Weeks later, the battalion was ordered to a reserve position, behind the regiment. There, it received replacement officers and men, while awaiting an order to move forward to fight again. The brief rest was welcome, for hunting is not sport when the hunters are also hunted.

On the second morning in reserve, Smith walked over to where MacKenzie was and said, "Come on over to the captain's tent. He wants to see us."

The two men walked the distance to the company commander's headquarters tent and announced themselves.

"Sergeants Smith and MacKenzie reporting as ordered sir," said Smith.

"Come on in," said Capt. Lauterbach, and the two untied and lifted a tent flap and entered, tying the flap behind them.

Capt. Lauterbach was seated behind a makeshift table that consisted of a board from a shipping crate with legs made fast with screws to each outer corner. The desk's inner side rested on his lap.

Capt. Lauterbach looked up, after the men had entered and come to attention before him, and said, "Stand easy. As y'all know, we lost two more commissioned officers and several more non-commissioned officers, during the last two months.

"Y'all also know we lost another battalion commander several days ago, when his jeep drove over a mine. As a result, I have been put in temporary command of battalion and have made necessary adjustments in the command structure.

"Lt. Bain of Company B's 2nd Platoon will temporarily command Company B. We have been assigned a new second lieutenant named Kowalski. He is an ROTC graduate from Michigan and is as ready to command a platoon as any newly fledged second lieutenant can be.

"Before I say more about Kowalski, I want to say something directly relating to y'all. Of the men that came to Korea, when this regiment was first moved here from Japan, you two are amongst the few that have survived unscathed and remain with it. During the long months we have been here, y'all have repeatedly distinguished yourselves, as riflemen and leaders. Because of that, you, Sgt. Smith, are now officially Company B's first sergeant, and you, Sgt. MacKenzie, are now officially a platoon sergeant. Congratulations and good luck.

"I want to say one more thing, and that is that Lt. Kowalski is expected here tomorrow. He will be assigned to 2nd Platoon, and I want you, MacKenzie, to keep him near you and give him whatever help you can, until he has been with us for a while and knows which regulations to follow and which to ignore. He is fresh out of officer training and has no combat experience.

"Taking over a first command will try any man. Since this is a combat unit, the lives of many men will depend upon what orders are given, when they are given, and how they are carried out. In officers' training, officer candidates are told to rely on their platoon sergeants until they know their men, the enemy, the terrain, the equipment, and the supplies and have enough experience to make safe decisions that weigh all of these. I am certain Lt. Kowalski will rely on you to help him through his first weeks here.

"We received another new second lieutenant today. His name is Wommack, and he will command Company B's 4th Platoon. He hails from near Sacramento, California, and is also fresh out of officers' training. I'll introduce him to his platoon sergeant in short order.

"I have left the task of choosing other replacement noncoms to each platoon commander. In the case of lieutenants Kowalski and Wommack, I will let them know their platoon sergeants are ready to help them. I am certain they will want to know who their platoon sergeants think are the best men to promote, and that they will get the best advice possible from each platoon sergeant.

"If, after we have been in a few more battles, our new officers are, God willing, yet alive and unharmed, they should be well blooded and able to make their own decisions.

"The new officers will be announced to the men today, through their noncoms. When I have an approved list of promotions to corporal, I'll have the platoon commanders pass the word to the men promoted and their units.

"Again, I congratulate you both. I wish I had a hundred men like y'all. The battalion would be as effective as a regiment, if I did."

With that, Capt. Lauterbach half stood, while holding on to papers on his desk with his left hand, and extended his right arm and shook hands with both Smith and MacKenzie.

"Thank you, sir," Smith and MacKenzie said, almost in unison.

"That is all for now, sergeants. I would like to see you Smith back here in an hour, with the battalion's noncoms that are not on duty. I want to brief y'all about what I have been told is going on at the front."

"Yes sir," the sergeants answered. They then untied the tent flap, stepped outside, retied the flap, and congratulated each other.

While in reserve, word was passed through the command chain that the army would begin to release to civilian life those men whose enlistments had expired. Amongst the discharge papers were those for Darden, whose cold, stiff body was now somewhere between the battalion and the US, on its way back to a Mississippi graveyard. MacKenzie felt the loss of a pal, as well as the irony of when Darden's discharge had come through. He had seen many men killed and killed many men, but Darden's death was very personal, and it seemed to wound and depress him. A trusted friend was gone, and he quietly grieved the loss.

Two days later, Smith, MacKenzie and several corporals headed towards a truck to get hot chow for breakfast. As they did, a messenger from Capt. Lauterbach strode up beside them and said, "Sgt. Smith., Capt. Lauterbach wants to see you, as soon as you can get over to his tent."

Smith wrinkled his brow and said, "I'll come right away."

To MacKenzie and the others he said, "I'll join y'all in a few minutes. Leave a little food for me when y'all go through the chow line, y'all hear?"

Then he turned and, accompanied by the message bearer, walked to Capt. Lauterbach's tent. He came out after only five minutes and ran into the chow tent where he walked up the chow line in a point beside MacKenzie, smiling as broadly as a jackass eating briars.

He slapped MacKenzie and the man next to him on their shoulders and said, "My discharge order came through. I'm going to leave y'all good buddies, but let's stay in touch. Yours should be here any day now. When y'all get out, maybe we can get together and enjoy a quiet day sitting on a porch in rocking chairs and reminiscing about Japan and this war."

"I'm happy for you," said MacKenzie, and this expression of good will was repeated by many of the other men, some of whom added that they could hardly wait until their turn came to head back to the US. The congratulatory statements were couched in the typical vernacular of enlisted men and laced with four-letter words describing the army, Korea, and Smith's "good luck."

MacKenzie grasped Smith gently by the upper part of the left arm and said, "You had best have something to eat now. If you don't, you're so excited you're going to burn off 10 pounds before the day is half over."

Smith laughed and joined them in the mess hall. After that, they sat on the cots in a tent and talked.

Capt. Lauterbach, Lt. Kowalski, MacKenzie, and many other officers and men of the battalion wished Smith well before he left. When he left for the replacement center several days later, MacKenzie and several members of the 2nd Platoon made it a point to be there to shake his hand, slap his back, and wish him farewell and good luck in civilian life.

As he moved towards the truck that would carry him and others southward, Smith said to MacKenzie, "You should be getting your rotation notice any day now. You've been here for long enough to be ordered to another duty station, for the final months of duty. Don't forget to look me up when you get out."

MacKenzie said he would, and each agreed to stay in touch with an occasional letter, until they met again in civilian life. Smith, with a broad smile on his face, then boarded the truck. He was smiling as the truck moved away and when it finally disappeared around a hill. MacKenzie and the men with him waved until the truck disappeared and then returned to their duties.

MacKenzie walked the short distance to Lt. Kowalski's tent, where he stated his presence and entered. Lt. Kowalski, who had sent for him, looked up from behind the little table he was at work at and said, "Hi, Mac. I understand you have been a good friend and advisor to several men. Just in case you thought no one knew, your satisfied friends give you a lot of quiet and positive publicity. You seem to have a bent for spreading spiritual comfort. Were you involved in that field, before you entered the army?"

"I was a pre-ministerial student and attended seminary in Georgia for a year, before I dropped out. Once I dropped out, I lost my draft exemption and was inducted into the army. The men found out about this, in casual conversation, when we were back in Japan. There was relatively little call for my thoughts back there, but the number of men that asked my opinion about their problems rose, after we came to Korea."

"You seem to be good at making the men that talk with you about their problems feel better. You seem to have a spiritual vocation. Why did you drop out of seminary?"

"My thinking about God began to change. I am no longer certain God is with us and answers prayers. I feel he is the creator and is in us in one way. That is, he built into us the ability to be happy and to heal ourselves of sicknesses. But other than that, I suspect God is only concerned with our spiritual well-being. That's not very comforting and not what my denomination wants its clergy to think."

"Do you believe that now?"

"The more I see of war, the more is seems true."

There was a pause, as the lieutenant thought. Then he said, "If you think that, how can you counsel men that want comforting thoughts that God is with them here in the midst of battle?"

"I do my best to ignore my thoughts, when I tell men how I would deal with a problem. I know most want to think God is a great candy machine in the sky, into which they can drop their prayers and have an answer to them come out. I do what a chaplain would do and deal with each man as each man wants to be dealt with."

"How do you know how they want to be dealt with?"

"I listen to them and ask questions that help me to understand each man's thoughts. That's the only way I know how to do it."

"It probably is the only way, unless you had a file about each that reported the man's religious beliefs, hopes, and fears. I wonder if chaplains deal with each man as individually as you do? Now, one last question. Why do you do it?"

"I have the ability to do this, and some men get comfort from the counsel I give them. I pray with those that want prayer and advise them about Bible readings and prayer. It may be considered hypocritical that I do this, or the emotional and spiritual help I give may be considered an act of good will and a good use of this talent. I don't know which and do not want to think about which it is. I just do my best to help the men that ask me for advice."

There was another pause, this time longer. Then the lieutenant told MacKenzie, "You're a good man, Mac. I'm sorry I asked so many personal questions, but I wondered about the stories I heard about what you do with some of your spare time. I really called you here to let you know a squad from each company is supposed to do a recon patrol tonight, and you have been designated to lead our patrol. Choose seven other men, and be back here at 1600 hours with the corporal you choose to go with you. I will review with you the order I received and show you all a map of the terrain you all are expected to cover.

"And here, take one of these," he said as he handed MacKenzie a chocolate bar. "My wife sent me a 'Care' package."

MacKenzie thanked the lieutenant and left to walk the distance to where the platoon was camped. On the way, only a minute later, he tried to break off a piece of chocolate. The chocolate bar snapped apart, sending a few bits onto the ground. In the short time he had been outside the tent, the chocolate, already cold when he was given it, had been frozen solidly by the temperature and wind.

He put the chocolate bit into his mouth and savored the delicious taste as it melted. When he reached the men's tents, he stopped here and there to talk with those present.

17

RESERVE AGAIN

The regiment was soon ordered to a rear area reserve position. On the second morning there, Lt. Col. Greer, the battalion's newest commanding officer, and his staff were in formation before the battalion headquarters tent, and the battalion was in a parade formation facing them. The colonel called the names of several men, including MacKenzie, and ordered them to present themselves before him. The order was relayed to the companies' ranks, and the men strode forward and halted, in a rank, facing the colonel and his staff.

The colonel walked in front of each man and there read a brief summary of the bravery for which the man had been cited. He then told each the medal that had been awarded him and entered in his service record. When he stepped before MacKenzie, he read the award citation that stated MacKenzie had been awarded the Silver Star for his initiative, leadership, and bravery leading attacks that destroyed entrenched Chinese positions, at the risk of his life, thereby enabling the battalion to continue its movement.

"Congratulations, sergeant," he said, in a normal speaking voice, "You are a good example for the men." And then, in almost a whisper, "I understand Lt. Kowalski reported you got him off to a great start as platoon commander."

When the colonel reached the rank's end he stepped back and, in a voice almost everyone present could hear, said, "You men are the finest examples of the fighting spirit and leadership ability that has kept our battalion together and effective, during the most dismal period the army has faced in Korea. We are proud of you and proud you wear our regimental emblem."

MacKenzie and the other men were then ordered to return to the formation.

The regiment sort of lollygagged for two weeks, while replacements joined it. During that time, some close order drill was the most extreme form of physical exertion required. In addition to men, equipment that was heavily used, or had been destroyed, was replaced. They got brand spanking new equipment, sticky with creosote that had to be cleaned off, and as much ammunition as they could bear or carry in their trucks and jeeps.

The comforts most immediately welcomed by the soldiers were hot showers, new clean winter uniforms, parkas, hats with pull-down ear covers that also covered behind the neck, heavy socks, and shoe packs. The old, worn uniforms and other clothing were left in heaps. And more than that, there were hot meals every day.

"By Gawd," said one soldier to MacKenzie, as they sat in a mess building eating a hot meal and drinking hot coffee. "Maybe we have died and gone to heaven. My uniform was so dirty it had grown onto me. I never though I would be able to peel it off. I forgot what a shower was, much less a hot one. And the food is better than I ever recall army food was. And there's clean bunks and a new winter uniform. I smell funny now. Sort of like a clothing store."

One of the Kentucky men, thinking out loud, said, "It's too bad we didn't get winter uniforms when winter first howled over us. All those frostbitten fingers and feet were so damned unnecessary. I'll bet men on occupation duty in Germany had extra, full-winter field clothing to hang in their lockers, in nice, warm barracks, while we got frost bit and some froze to death."

"Aw, knock it off, Holcomb," a man from West Virginia said. "You know the gu'mint don't care. There's a lot more like we uns where we come from."

"What on airth do you say," said another man. "Why, the US guv'mint knows they ain't nothing too good fo' the 'Mer'kin sojeh."

"Yup, exactly raht," came the answer. "They is sartin nothin' is too good fo' us, so they giv' us nothin' but damned poor brass, right up till Ridgway jined us."

"Ah reckon yo'r raht, but don't want to say so definitively yet. I want to cogitate a bit, till mah brain thaws. Ah have sot here fur half an hour, eatin' hot chow and awonderin' about what we bin through. What you say has a true ring to it, but I ain't truly certain. I'd best get more hot coffee. When mah brain has thawed properly, in a few more days, ah'll decide if yo'r raht."

During a lull in training one day, MacKenzie and several corporals from his platoon sat and lay on the ground talking. One of the corporals said to him, "Sarge, you must be long overdue for rotation out of Korea. You should have left Korea at about the same time as Sgt. Smith, right? Have you said something to the lieutenant?"

"You should have been discharged by now, right?" said another corporal.

"No. I'm not overdue for rotation or discharge. I had my time extended by six months, so I could stay with you bozos and try to keep you all from getting drilled through by Chinese bullets."

"Mighty kind of you Uncle Mac, but we can take care of ourselves. You need someone to care for you, or you wouldn't have extended your time here."

"You must be crazy," another man said. "Why didn't you tell us? We could have talked you out of it."

"It did not seem appropriate to say anything. I reckoned it would be apparent eventually."

"What were you thinking of that made you extend? I'd be out of here in the blink of an eye, if I had the chance."

"I was offered officer training. That got me to thinking again about civilian life and what I would do back there. I am not certain I want it. Instead, I extended my enlistment. It gives me time to think about officer training."

"But why? Jeez, sarge, if'n yuz had sed sumpin' Ahy-duh told yuz why yuz wuz better off headin' home," said D'Angelo, who hailed from the Bronx, in New York City.

"I was tempted to accept officers' training, but want time to cogitate about it. That's why I decided to extend my enlistment, instead. I was told the offer is good, if I decide I want it. Maybe the army would be a good career. I reckon I have a job to do here and know what it is. I don't yet know what I want to do, if I go back home again."

"Sgt. Smit' told us yuz wuz studyin' t' be a preacher, before yuz got drafted. Yuz does a good job wit yer ministry her, why not go back and finish yer studies and be a minister?"

"I'm not certain I am the right person for that career, but I am certain I have a job to do here. I'm all right here."

"It ain't dat good here," said Sobieski, a tall solidly build corporal from Green Point, in Brooklyn. "It's paradise back home, in Green Pernt, compared wit' here. I'd like t' be anywer' in det states, 'stead of here. Yes, sir. If'n deh army told me my time wuz up, I'd be out of here so fast all youz guys'd see is a green streak. I'd get a job and do watever woik I could find, an' in my free time I'd have my goil in one hand and a beer in deh udder. Dat's deh good life! And youz sure as hell can't have dat here."

"To tell you the truth Sobieski, I hadn't quite thought about free time activity back home in quite the colorful way you do. If I had, I would have gone back. Instead, because my outlook is more limited than yours, I did what I felt most comfortable doing. I reckoned I have gotten into the stride of this war and can do more good here than I would do back stateside. Besides, I don't know yet what I want to do when I go back, or if I want to go back to civilian life."

"You should at least have taken officer training. Yeah! Yuz would uv been out of here and probably gotten a billet in Europe or stateside, once yuz wuz a second louie (lieutenant)," said D'Angelo.

"That is worth considering."

"Well here yuz can be platoon sergeant an' a off-duty sky pilot, at deh same time," said Sobieski. "Were else can yuz get a job description like dat?"

"Yup! Where else?" said MacKenzie, as he chuckled over the men's comments.

On February 21st, the battalion began to move northward, as part of Operation Killer. It took only until March 1st for Ridgway to close the UN line south of the Han River. In the process, the Chinese were driven northward with huge losses. Ridgway got his troops in line, and ensured each unit set up its defense in depth and took the right precautions against infiltration. Then he had artillery and aircraft fire devastating amounts of ordnance at the Chinese facing his troops. Once that was done, the UN forces moved northward again.

After Killer, came Operation Ripper, which took the regiment, in the central part of the front, to a new line called Idaho Line. As Ripper moved forward, it became inevitable UN forces would drive north of Seoul, and the Communist forces left without a fight. MacKenzie heard from someone that was with US troops that moved into Seoul, that what was left of it consisted of some tin-roofed shanties and only two or three civic buildings amidst otherwise total ruin.

MacKenzie listened to a private from his platoon tell him the latest rumor, which MacKenzie had also heard from his company commander, who had heard it from the battalion commander. "Believe it or not, Sarge, the North Koreans are back and fighting in division strength again," said the man. "There are reportedly several of their divisions in the hills east of us attacking South Korean units. I also heard there was one whole North Korean division behind our lines, in the southwestern sector, carrying out guerrilla warfare. It was there until our lines solidified and began to beat the Chinese northward. Then it rammed through a South Korean position and escaped northward.

"Amazing how Tokyo can't count how many enemy are killed. They told us the number of North Korean dead, and that number was the same as the number of North Korean troops they said there was when the war began. Now there are North Korean divisions fighting again. If the number of NKPA killed is what the UN high command said was killed, then North Korea does not have a large enough population to allow it to train and field more divisions that soon."

MacKenzie nodded and said, "Yup. I heard the same reports. Seems as if someone in Tokyo can't add the body counts in field reports properly."

"I think they bin lying for to get good publicity in the states," the soldier said. "They want to continue this war and won't be allowed to, if they tell the truth. It seems like someone in Tokyo bin bullshitting us but good."

"You make a good case," MacKenzie said.

"The sky is overcast again today and it's damned cold. I reckon this winter will never end," said another soldier who had listened to their conversation.

"What goes on?" MacKenzie asked, as he and the other men noticed a long line of small Korean men, clad in military uniforms walk forlornly into the battalion's perimeter. With them were several Korean army officers.

"They're called Katusas," said Lt. Kowalski, who had just walked within earshot of them. "Katusa is short for Korean Augmentation Troops US Army. We've been given them to help fill in our ranks and make use of some of the draftable men the Korean army can't properly use. At least that is what I've been told. Each platoon in the regiment will be assigned about six of them. I also heard the reason we've been given them is that the army thinks that by putting Koreans into our ranks, they will learn how to fight better than they would in Korean regiments. We are supposed to somehow make them into soldiers and integrate them into the ranks with us."

"Damn!" said MacKenzie. "Some of them are just young teenagers."

The subject of Katusas was raised weeks later, at a meeting of Capt. Lauterbach and his platoon commanders and sergeants. One lieutenant complained that many of the Katusas were probably only 14 or 15 years old, and most seemed weak and completely untrained in military discipline or weapons use.

"Sir, some of them try to understand what we try to have them do and then try to do it with us," said one lieutenant. "The others seem less able or willing to try. The only tasks we have given them that they can do with some reliability is entrenching, carrying supplies, and similar work. No one wants one of them next to him in a combat situation, because we are certain there will be no one beside us the moment a battle begins."

"Your assessment of them appears to be right, and I know how we use them," said the captain, "but we received a reminder from regiment that our job is to make soldiers out of them. They can give us added firepower, if we can integrate them into our units. I want each of y'all to try to communicate with them, by example. They are bright young men and will respond. If we treat them as if they are not competent, they will respond accordingly and meet our low expectation. Try to think of them as young men that can help us."

"We've tried to communicate with them, sir," said a platoon sergeant, "but that's easier to order done than to do. None of us know Korean, and none of them know English. How can we integrate them into our ranks, if we can't communicate with them?"

"It does make them less useful than the army means for them to be," said the captain.

"Useful!" said a lieutenant. "Why, sir, it sometimes makes them downright dangerous for us. If we use them as soldiers we will have untrained, armed boys in our midst and will not know what their reactions will be when we get into a fire fight. We have not been able to communicate with them by example or with words, because they have almost no way to know what we want to communicate to them. That has caused some dangerous situations.

"Let me give you an example, sir. When my squad was on its way back from a patrol in front of our position, the men had to watch our Katusas and sometimes hold up their rifle barrels to be sure they didn't accidently shoot us. I'd like to talk with the damned desk jockey that thought up this arrangement."

"Unfortunately, there's nothing we can do about the Katusas. Every other army unit has the same problem. We must make the best of it. Do the best y'all can with them."

That was the last time Capt. Lauterbach mentioned the subject of integrating Katusas into combat ranks.

18

AT THE FRONT

The battalion was in a position towards the Central Front, awaiting orders to move forward, to the rear, or to a flank. In the bitterly chilly, sunless midday, a line of small, white clad men, bent forward by the heavy load each carried on his back, moved forward at a steady pace into the battalion's perimeter. They had walked for miles from the south to reach the battalion.

"They're a welcome sight," said a soldier. "Our ammo is runnin' low. I hope they brung chow and ammo."

"Them Korean porters work like mules," said a corporal who had joined the battalion only weeks before.

"They surely do, but back home, we took a lot better care of our mules than the Korean government takes of them porters."

"They certainly do work hard and seem to be the worse for the work they do," said MacKenzie. "They've been working just as hard as they did when they were first assigned to supply duty several months ago. The word is they are forced laborers. They work as porters because the Korean government has ordered them to do so.

"We have about 40 of them. They carry crucial supplies for us to use and have been particularly important here in this hilly terrain. But they do take a beating. Of the 40 or so of them the company was first assigned, not 10 are left. The rest were killed, captured, wounded, or deserted. Most of the porters you all see are men the South Korean government assigned to replace the missing ones. They are just as young and undernourished as the first ones, and they work like mules every day, except for occasions when they do heavy work in camp."

MacKenzie interrupted his talk with the men and turned quickly to look behind him. "What's that racket about?" he shouted.

A corporal strode quickly to him and said, "A Korean officer showed up and took one of the Katusas from Company A with him. He must have had an order that allowed him to take the kid yonder, to that open area behind our line and make him dig a shallow trench. Then we saw him shoot the kid in the head and kick the body into the trench.

"The men that saw it happen are furious. None of them knows why the kid was killed, and word about what happened spread like wildfire. If Capt. Lauterbach and several officers from our battalion had not happened by just as the ROK officer killed the boy, I reckon some of our men would have shot that ROK officer dead. In fact, I know they would have."

A soldier near them said, "Sometimes, I wonder what good it does for us to be here. These people are so damned brutal and uncivilized to each other. What difference does it make which side wins? The brutality will go on anyway."

"It's almost April," said a soldier. "I bin here for long enough to get out. I reckon the damned army plumb forgot about me."

"They ain't forgot you, Morrison," a man near him said, "They just don't give a shit. You might as well pick out a place here where you want to retire, or be buried."

"Some overweight headquarters noncom or private has my discharge order on his desk and is probably too busy polishing his shoes for a dress parade, or leave, to bother with it."

"Exactly where are we?" one of the men asked MacKenzie.

"We're a little north of the 38th parallel again, and fighting in North Korea."

"It don't smell no different to me than it did south of the 38th parallel," said the soldier who asked the question, and the other men laughed.

"The smell is everywhere, in Korea," said MacKenzie. "Why gripe about it. It's the Korean smell. We've had it in our nostrils since we came here. They use human shit and piss to fertilize their fields. Some of the men that were in the unit, when it made its first retreat, waded through rice paddies to make their escape. They rejoined us, but we smelled them acoming, before we saw them. They claimed they had that stink in their noses for a month after they finally were able to shower and get clean uniforms. I mean to tell you all, they were a ripe-smelling bunch of dog faces for a while. I reckon we could have put them out in forward positions and, if the wind was away from us, the North Koreans would have stayed away."

"Not much chance," said a man that listened to the conversation. "Those gooks are used to the smell. They were borned to it and growed up with it. It's the smell of home to them."

The soldiers laughed.

Then one said, "I reckon we could use the Korean smell to lure the enemy into ambushes. They're so used to it they might think we wus one of their own units. It could be a kind of a camouflage."

MacKenzie smiled and nodded agreement. "That might work. We really could smell them a few hundred feet away, when the wind was right. On a dark night we could have smelled them before we saw them."

"I don't believe that," said another man. "The whole country stinks so badly it ain't possible to smell a few soldiers that's bin dunked in shit and piss."

"I reckon the fact that the men are above ground level and moving often does make the smell more detectable," another man said.

"What about the after shave and cologne our men use?" said another man. "What about the cigarettes most men smoke? Don't you think the enemy can smell us too, when the wind is right?"

"Those smells are probably overwhelmed by the stink around us. I know my nose can't pick out our smell from the overall stink."

"That's your nose. You're used to our own smell. The gooks aren't and can probably smell the differences between us and them."

MacKenzie was no longer listening to the conversation. Instead, he had taken out his *Guide to Korea* and found the pages with maps of the peninsula. The maps were out-line maps and showed only major towns, rivers, and roads. He beckoned the men to him.

"Look," he said, "we are here somewhere, near Uijongbu, which should lie about here, just north of Seoul. It is a center for the Commies' communications networks and supply routes."

"You reckon Ridgway's goin' to ram us through the Chinese and North Koreans and on to the Yalu again, sarge?"

"I don't know," said MacKenzie. "We can only wait and see."

"We bin stopped and told to dig in," said a soldier.

"Yup," MacKenzie said in agreement. "Ridgway calls our positions part of 'The Kansas Line'. Sounds mighty fine. One of the men said he heard a report that our part of the line stretches from the Imjin, in the west, to Hwachon Reservoir, in the middle of the peninsula. If that's right, then the whole UN line from the western to eastern coasts is about 115 miles long. It will be a lot easier for us to defend it than to advance northward. The peninsula widens greatly the farther north one moves, and the mountains mid-peninsula would prevent easy contact between a force on the eastern side and one on the western side. We already tried that, and it was a disaster. If Ridgway's the general I think he is, I reckon he found a lesson in that disaster and will not try the same thing."

The regiment prepared defensive positions that were almost permanent looking. All along the front there were forward positions manned by a few men, with barbed wire around them, except for escape paths. Nearer to the regiment's main line were similar positions, but more of them.

"Looks like a World War I battle field on the Western Front," said MacKenzie.

"Why do you say that?" said the soldier next to him.

"These trenches and bunkers and barbed wire are the reason," said MacKenzie. "That's the way the First World War was fought, on the Western Front. It was trench warfare and the front stretched from the North Sea to Switzerland."

MacKenzie's platoon was part of the inner defense line, between the outer line and the main line.

Lt. Kowalski came by and showed MacKenzie a map of the area immediately in front of them. "This is our third day here. Two squads from your platoon have been assigned to patrol Sector Two, over here, in the forward area, tonight. I want you to lead them. If you run into the enemy, engage them and call for reinforcements. We want to ascertain if they have moved in ahead of us in force."

MacKenzie led the patrol out through the platoon's forward line, after darkness fell. They moved carefully along a path that led between mine fields and barbed wire, following a light-colored strip laid down for them to follow. They were challenged by one of the unit's forward positions, and then allowed to continue on towards no-man's land, which lay between their forward positions and the enemy's forward positions.

A platoon leader briefs his men, before they leave on a reconnaissance patrol.
U.S. Army photo

The patrol had moved less than a mile north the battalion's northernmost position when it met a Chinese patrol moving towards it. Neither side knew the other was in the area, until one spotted the other and began to fire at it with small arms. The US patrol, with better small unit coordination and superior fire power quickly got the upper hand and drove the surviving Chinese back to a hill to the north, where they disappeared. Two GIs had been wounded in the skirmish and several Chinese were known killed, their bodies left, as the Chinese retreated. By the time the skirmish ended, the GIs were mostly in an open area south of the hill.

Now, small arms fire from the hill began to splatter around the GIs. The Chinese, protected by darkness, had MacKenzie and his men in an exposed situation, and he ordered his men to withdraw to less exposed positions, while firing at every point from which they could see shots coming from.

From two points on the hill, about 200 yards from him, machine guns now fired on the GIs, and the men were pinned flat on the ground with almost nothing to hide behind. Tracers in the stream of bullets from the Chinese machine guns showed the Chinese where their rounds struck and showed the GIs from where the Chinese rounds were fired. MacKenzie crawled sideways, flat on his belly, to his radioman and called Lt. Kowalski to ask for artillery fire on the Chinese-held hill and give map coordinates for his and the enemy's positions.

The men waited motionless, but no artillery fire came. The area behind them was flat and had very few bushes. If they moved, they would be easy targets. Only by lying still could they hope to avoid detection.

After what seemed to MacKenzie to be an hour, but was actually 20 minutes, a tank and the rest of Company B's 2nd Platoon moved along the valley and joined them. The tank began to fire its main gun at one of the Chinese machine gun positions. Its third shot hit right on the gun emplacement, and an explosion lit the night sky for a moment revealing what appeared to be stone, dirt, body parts, and equipment flying into the air.

"Damned good shot!" shouted one of MacKenzie's men. "Damned good shot."

MacKenzie jumped to his feet and ran to the tank's rear, where he picked up the intercom phone and gave information to guide the tank gunner's aim to the other Chinese machine gun.

From his standing position behind the tank, MacKenzie could see several of his men had rolled over onto their backs. He knew that meant they had been badly wounded, for only a badly wounded soldier rolls over on his back. It is a position in which a wounded man can breathe more easily than when lying on his belly.

On his left, along the line where the hill met the valley floor, he saw Lt. Kowalski leading two squads of 2nd Platoon through bushes that provided some cover. MacKenzie ran, half crouching, back to his former position, ahead of the two squads he led out on patrol. As he ran by one man, the soldier, on his back and bleeding profusely from his side and groin, said, "God, help me! Sarge, I've been hit. I've been hit. Help me!"

It was Johnson, the young harmonica player from Kentucky, who had been so happy last November about his newly born son. MacKenzie could not stop. That was the rule. Wounded men had to be left for the medics and combat-fit soldiers had to continue their attack.

MacKenzie ran on to a point ahead of the patrol and nearer the Chinese-held hill than any other man in the patrol. Then, he half turned towards his men and shouted loudly, "Everyone up! Follow me!" As he shouted, he motioned to them with his left arm to come with him towards the enemy positions.

He saw men rise from the ground and start towards him. Then he turned and began to run towards the enemy. As he ran, the ground under him shook, and he felt an intense bolt of flaming heat along much of his body.

His forward motion stopped, and he fell onto his right knee. In the space of two or three seconds, he tried to open his right hand, which gripped the rifle stock at the narrow grip-point behind the trigger housing. It would not move, for blood from a wound he had not noticed had frozen his hand there.

He tried to steady himself by gripping the rifle with his left hand, towards the muzzle, and use the rifle as a lever to raise himself. As he tried to rise, the hill ahead of him and the night around him became grey and then white and then a million pin-pricks of light flashed in his eyes. Within seconds, he fell forward onto his face and left side and lay motionless on the ice and stone. He was not aware of anything   else.

EPILOGUE

Korean War Casualties

About 725,000 US servicemen served in Korea during the war. Of these, 22,300 were killed in action, another 10,300 died as a result of accidents, 103,248 were wounded in combat, 3,746 were captured, and 8,142 remain missing in action. A disproportionate number of these losses happened during or before the period covered in this book.

Other UN nations contributed about 150,000 military personnel to fight alongside US and South Korean forces. The largest contingents were sent by the United Kingdom, which contributed 60,000 men, Canada 27,000, and Australia 18,423. Altogether, other UN forces suffered 18,423 casualties (3,360 killed in action, 11,886 wounded, 1,801 missing in action, and 1,376 taken prisoner). The largest proportion of these losses also happened during or before the period covered in this book.

The number of men who served in the Republic of Korea's military was not found by the author. However, South Korean forces suffered about 684,000 casualties. Of these, 227,800 were killed in action; 429,000 wounded; and 13,000 missing in action and thought to have been tortured to death or executed by North Korean soldiers, or to have died of starvation or mistreatment while prisoners. Only 7,142 South Korean troops survived captivity.

Instances were documented of the NKPA murdering US servicemen they captured. What is not known is the total number of US and other UN troops reported missing in action that were actually captured and then murdered by North Korean troops. One million South Korean civilians are estimated to have been killed during the war, including many thousands murdered by the NKPA.

The number of men that fought in the NKPA during the war is not known. However, the NKPA suffered an estimated 520,000 casualties, mostly before the period covered by this book. The total includes an estimated 406,000 killed, 114,000 wounded, and 95,531 captured. One million North Korean civilians may also have been killed during the war.

About 130,000 Communist Chinese soldiers entered the war initially, and Chinese troop strength probably reached from 200,000 to 250,000 men. It has been estimated that another 150,000 Chinese served as porters to carry supplies to Chinese troops in Korea. China's losses have been estimated at 600,000 men killed, 716,000 wounded, and 21,400 Chinese troops captured. Frostbite was a major cause of Chinese casualties. The greatest number of Chinese losses happened after the period covered by this book.

From June to November 1950 (before the period covered by this book), the NKPA was in total charge of all US, ROK, and UN war prisoners (POWs). Many POWs died from harsh treatment during that time. POW camps were created, by the NKPA, in November 1950, and their administration was taken over by the Chinese army in mid-December 1950.

From spring 1951 on, the Chinese army had sole charge of POW camps, except those for South Korean war prisoners, which the NKPA continued to administer. Conditions in Chinese-administered POW camps began to improve during the summer of 1951. They continued to improve until the US-UN and Chinese-North Koreans exchanged war prisoners from August through September 1953.

ABOUT THE AUTHOR

Norman Philip Black was raised in the Gravesend section of Brooklyn, New York.

He served as a US Navy Journalist in the western Pacific; reported for United Press International and edited copy for the Associated Press, both in New York City; and then worked as a reporter for the Newark (New Jersey) Evening and Sunday News. He later worked in public relations, financial relations, and governmental relations for Fortune 500 companies, as well as for a privately-owned corporation.

Mr. Black's news stories, feature articles and commentaries have appeared in newspapers and magazines in many countries. He holds a diploma from the U.S. Navy's Journalist "A" School; the degrees of B.A. and of M.S. in Education from Wagner College; and an M.S. degree from Columbia University's Graduate School of Journalism, which he attended on a full scholarship.

Made in the USA
Charleston, SC
26 March 2012